The
Affair

Acknowledgements

Thank you to my family for always believing in me and supporting my dreams, no matter how crazy they are. I love you.

I also want to say how much I appreciate my Beta Readers for all of their help, hard work and dedication (K.M. Keeton, Angelica Charles and R. D.)

Also, a very special thank you to my dear friend and fellow Author Fran Comesanas for all of your help and insight while writing this book and making Vincent come alive.

One more thank you to Kateryna Kimbrough for your help with translating English into Ukrainian.

Prologue

Vincent

My life has always been predictable. I conformed to the rules, made the correct decisions and when I look back, I can be proud of what I have accomplished. On the surface, you can say I have it all. I am a very successful lawyer and was offered to take over the firm a few years back. I have been married to my wife Michelle for nearly twenty-six years and we have two wonderful sons, Luke and David. Our boys are now in their twenties and have their own families. I was also blessed with two beautiful grandchildren, a girl named Libby and a boy named Jackson. So now you may ask yourself, why would I consider an affair?

If you dig a little deeper, things are never as they seem. My marriage had run its course, I hardly ever see my wife. Michelle is either busy with her friends or involved in the community. I can't blame her. Early in my career I had to spend a lot of time at the office or away from home so she built a life without me. Things were still fine when the boys were home. We would find time to do things together as a family, anything from baseball games to concerts. Now that it's just the two of us, it seems that family bond left with the kids. Intimacy is something that happens very rarely, we just don't have the same drive. One thing that really bothers me is that I don't feel a connection to her. I do love her of course, but it's not the love we used to share for one another.

Over the years, I had come to terms with the way we led our life. Any amount of conversation and even counseling didn't 'fix' us. After every session, things would improve for a few days until they returned to the way they were before. I still remember that hefty bill. I would have been better off donating the money to a charity. Well, they say you should never regret anything and even though it didn't work, at least we did try.

Little did I know that one July morning would change the course of my entire life. Our firm had been trying to fill the secretary position for the last month and my colleagues and I were so relieved when we finally found someone. She was a thirty-four-year-old woman with long dark brown hair, green eyes and an unbelievable body. One smile from Shelby Hunter and I could feel myself melting. I know exactly what you're thinking. Here's this guy going through the typical midlife crisis, hoping to have some fun with a younger woman. That was never the case and all I ask is that you read my story before judging me too harshly.

Chapter One

Vincent

Here's a little background on me. I grew up in New York, Brooklyn to be exact. My father, Robert, was a jack of all trades, working since he was fourteen years old, and my mother, Irina, stayed home with us four kids. My mother's family immigrated to the United States from the Ukraine back in the twenties. Even though they left their country, they made sure to keep their heritage alive by surrounding themselves with fellow Ukrainians. One day, my father delivered a package to my grandparent's home and my mother answered the door. As soon as they locked eyes he was mesmerized and knew that he wanted to spend the rest of his life with her. It wasn't all smooth sailing though. My grandparents didn't approve of my father. They had planned for my mother to marry within the close-knit community but eventually, he was able to win them over. They married within a year and nine months later my brother Robert Junior came along. I also have two older sisters, making me the baby of the family. Growing up, we were far from rich but we had something that money couldn't buy, love and a strong unity. I always admired my parents bond. The way they look at each other, the way my father always kisses my mother's forehead, the way she holds his hand. It's always as if it were the first time every time. They are both well into their seventies but are very healthy and I thank God, every day.

Growing up, I was fairly reserved. I loved to read, and doing well in school was very important. I always had excellent grades, and luckily it came easy to me. My sisters Alla and Marina were always more into boys, hair, and makeup which drove my mother insane. At least they ended up putting all of their practice to good use. They both became hairdressers and actually opened up their own salon about fifteen years ago. Our mother is their number one customer. Robert is … well he's unique to say the least. There is not one word to describe him. He's always been very outgoing, popular and women flock to him. He owns a large car dealership in Queens and is currently on wife number four. He has a going joke, after every divorce he says that it was a test drive and he's still searching for the right one. Well, he just turned fifty-six, if he hasn't found her by now, I don't think he will.

I met my wife Michelle in college. She had a dream of becoming a nurse and I was on my path to achieve my goal of becoming a lawyer. Within four months of dating we learned that Michelle became pregnant and decided to get married as soon as possible. Even though this wasn't the way we envisioned our life to start out, we loved each other and started preparing for the birth of our first child.

A few months later, our son Luke was born and it was one of the best moments in my entire life. Holding him for the first time is something I will never forget. Michelle put her education on hold to take care of Luke and things seemed to be going very well. David followed three years later, completing our family. I just started law school the year our first son was born and looking back I must say those were some rough times. All of those long nights studying and preparing while Michelle tended to our boys. I finally graduated at twenty-seven and I thought things would settle down a bit, boy was I wrong. I was hired on with a small firm that I now own with a partner. In the early years, being the new guy, a lot of work came my way which made my home life a little difficult at times. Michelle was ready to start school again but since my schedule could be unpredictable it was hard to coordinate things.

I remember one particular night as if it were yesterday. She had just put the boys to bed and wanted to talk about *'the plan'*. When I didn't have any concrete answers, she lost it. I'm talking smashing plates on the floor. She didn't say a word and walked away towards our bedroom. I was shocked, she had always been very mellow most of the time and this behavior was completely foreign. I knew I had to do something. I wanted her to go back to school because I knew how important it was to her. Talking to my mother the next day, she volunteered to help out with Luke and David whenever we needed her. That was such a blessing, I know we couldn't have done it without her. The boys loved spending time with their grandparents and my wife was happy.

When Michelle finally completed nursing school she was hired at the hospital near our house, working in the maternity ward. In the first few years she had to work alternating shifts and my parents were there to help out with the kids again. Eventually she transferred to a Family Practice clinic and kept *'normal hours'*. I think it was the best decision she ever made, even though my family was there to support us, Luke and David missed having mom around, and she missed them.

Even though we led very busy lives we made sure to take a family vacation every year. Those were the times we definitely splurged going to places like the Bahamas, Hawaii, Canada, Europe and Australia. About eight years ago we took a trip to the Ukraine along with my parents and siblings. Since my mother was born in the United States it was wonderful for her to see where her family came from. That was a great trip and Michelle and the boys really enjoyed themselves as well. On that same trip we also visited a few places in Italy.

Michelle and I took a two-day trip to Venice. I thought it would be nice for just the two of us to getaway since I had noticed us drifting apart a bit. Thinking back, I wish I had never taken that trip with her. She complained about everything the entire time and nothing I did would make her happy. When we got back to New York I suggested we try counseling and after a few weeks of hesitation, she finally agreed. Like I said before, the counseling didn't help us so I'm not going to get into that. We just learned how to coexist together. We always respected each other but the passion and love had disappeared.

Fast forward to today, our lives revolve around a tight schedule. On Monday evenings Michelle's book club comes to the house and they discuss whatever romance novel they read the week before. Tuesday and Wednesday, she prepares things for the community meeting which takes place every Thursday after she gets off work. Friday nights are dedicated to her work colleagues, they usually catch a movie, go to dinner or have coffee. The grandkids come over on Saturdays, leaving Sundays open for me, unless the neighbor comes by. When Betty comes over, she may as well move in. We always have the hardest time getting her to leave. I know Michelle is just being polite because the two of them have absolutely nothing in common and there have been many times we have dodged her by quickly getting into the car and leaving. This really isn't the life I thought I would have but I guess it's the choices we made that have led us to where we are now.

When I left work on Friday, John, my partner told the team that we would have a new secretary starting on Monday. I usually interview the new hires but my schedule took me out of town when the interviews took place. I've seen her resume and it's outstanding. She's worked as a legal assistant before which will definitely be an asset. Our firm isn't very big but we are very successful and stay busy. John and I have two other associates and two paralegals, making us a six-person team. Well, seven if you count Ms. Hunter who will be joining us. I honestly had no idea just how important a secretary really is until we lost our last one on short notice.

Sitting in my office there's a knock at the door and John steps in with a beautiful young woman, donning a gorgeous smile.

"Hey Vince," he says leading her in my office. "This is Shelby Hunter, our new secretary."

I get up from my chair and come around the desk to shake her hand, she's even more beautiful up close. Those green eyes are magical.

"Ms. Hunter, my name is Vincent Steele. It's a pleasure to make your acquaintance," I say, trying my best to focus on her face and not her plunging neckline.

"It's great to meet you Mr. Steele. You can call me Shelby," she replies with a grin, making me smile.

"So Vince, I am going to give Shelby a quick tour of the office and introduce her to everyone else, "John begins. "Do you have the file for Mrs. Williams handy? I'd like to show her a few things so she can get familiar with some of the paperwork we use."

Chuckling I grab the file out of my desk. Mrs. Williams has been a longtime client and seeks legal advice for anything imaginable. This is actually her second file and it was quite smart of John to use her for some on the job training. As they leave my office I look up and right at that moment, Shelby turns around, giving me one last smile before disappearing. All I can say is wow. She is absolutely stunning. Let's just hope that there's a brain behind those good looks as well.

I don't have any appointments scheduled for today and it gives me time to catch up on a few files. Looking at my watch I notice it is 2 p.m. and I completely missed lunch. I'm not really hungry anyway but I figure it's a good time to get up and stretch my legs. I walk out of my office and see Shelby sitting at the reception desk. For a moment, I stand there and watch her. She is completely engrossed in a file, taking notes on a pad next to her. She looks so focused so I decide not to disturb her. What would I say anyway? Talk about the weather?

When the day is over I grab my blazer and briefcase, making my way out of my office. Walking past the reception desk, Shelby looks up and smiles, "Have a wonderful evening Mr. Steele."

"You too, Shelby," I reply before walking out.

When I get home, I walk inside towards my home office, setting my briefcase on the desk before making my way to the bedroom to change clothes. As I unbutton my shirt Michelle comes walking in.

"Hi Honey, how was work today?" she asks, carrying in a stack of laundry.

"It was great. We have a new secretary so we no longer have to take phone calls or schedule appointments ourselves."

"That's wonderful, I'm surprised it took so long to fill the position," she comments. "By the way, we are having meatloaf tonight. The girls from the club are coming a bit early so I asked them to join us for dinner."

"That should be fun," I reply, with a little sarcasm.

"Come on Vince, maybe broaden your horizons a bit. Don't you ever get sick of reading those mystery novels?" Michelle asks and I grin.

"Michelle, I don't think you will get me into reading romance books," I respond, removing my shirt and grabbing a polo shirt out of the closet.

"Well, currently we are reading a very interesting one about the civil war. You'll hear all about it at dinner," Michelle says.

"Looking forward to it, who all will be joining us?" I ask since normally the group is quite large.

"It's just going to be Miranda, Rebecca and Tracy tonight, that's why I figured they could come to dinner."

Those are the three I actually like, some of the other women seem a little stuck up, as if they are something better. Miranda and Michelle have been friends for close to ten years now. They met at a school function when the kids were younger. Miranda was the one that actually got Michelle into reading. Once in a while we are invited to Miranda's home for dinner and her husband, Phil, and I get along great as well. Phil is a dentist, our dentist actually, and one of the most generous people I have ever met. He would literally give someone the shirt off his back if asked. Anyhow, even though I'm not into their genre of books, I'm sure dinner will be interesting.

About an hour later, everyone arrives and we sit at the dining table to enjoy the wonderful food Michelle has made. Michelle is an excellent cook, always has been. Even when attempting a new recipe, she usually hits it out of the park, same goes for baking. Just as I assumed, the dinner conversation is quite…interesting. I will say, after hearing their discussion I may just decide to pick that book up and give it a try when I get a chance. After dinner, the ladies retreat into our living room and I clear the table and clean the kitchen. As I start the dishwasher, the phone rings and I go to answer it. Yes, we still have a regular house phone, hard to imagine in these times. I pick up and it's Luke, asking if I would be able to watch Libby on Thursday evening while he and Ashley go to dinner for their anniversary.

Libby is our first grandchild and she is a little sweetheart. She just turned four and her favorite pastime is putting clips into my hair and playing teatime. Knowing Michelle will be at the community meeting, I agree and Luke thanks me about ten times before hanging up. This will be their second anniversary. They didn't do things say the 'traditional' way since Libby came before they got married but nowadays, those things don't seem to matter much.

I sit down in our family room and turn on the news to see what is going on in the world. About an hour later Miranda, Rebecca and Tracy peek in to say goodbye and Michelle walks them to the door. It's only nine, but I keep finding myself nodding off so I turn off the TV, get up and head towards the bedroom. After brushing my teeth, I change clothes and slip into bed. Michelle joins me about ten minutes later, asking what I thought about their book discussion. Telling her I would consider actually reading it brings a smile to her face. I wasn't lying when I said it sounded interesting but I'm actually mainly considering reading it because I saw Michelle so passionate about it. We hardly have anything in common anymore so maybe this is something that can bring us closer together. It's worth a shot.

As soon as I get to the office the next day I don't see Shelby at her desk. In the back of my mind I figure she's probably late, young people never seem to have a sense of time. Setting my briefcase next to my desk I sit in the chair and a minute later there's a knock on the doorframe. I look up to find a smiling Shelby with a cup of coffee in her hand.

"Good morning Mr. Steele. I hope you are well rested. I went over your schedule and it looks like you have a busy day ahead of you. I've made you some coffee. John said you take it black," she says walking toward my desk.

For a moment I am speechless, that pencil skirt and blouse envelopes her body in a way that shouldn't be legal, and those stilettos. She looks sexy but very professional at the same time. Getting coffee served is something new. I drink it every morning but Maggie never did that for us. I could definitely get used to this.

"Thank you, Shelby. Yes, black is perfect," I respond as she hands me the cup. "When you get a chance, could you please pull the files for my afternoon appointments?"

"Already done, they are right there," she responds, pointing to the left of my desk.

"Wow, thank you," I say and she smiles.

"You're welcome Mr. Steele. I will be at my desk if you need anything else," she replies before walking out.

Grabbing the first file off the stack, I open the folder, finding a few sticky notes on the first page. Shelby wrote down the time of the appointment, their last visit, a quick summary of what was discussed and a few other helpful tidbits. She has beautiful handwriting and I really wonder when she found the time to do all of this. It's only her second day but I must say I am impressed, let's see if she can keep it up.

Chapter Two

Vincent

Shelby has been with us for about two weeks now and I'm still impressed with her. She is always on time, actually, even early on most days, organized and a pleasure to be around. Her smile is contagious and her interaction with the clients is very professional. Everyone is getting along great and she's really integrated well. I've noticed John has been lingering around her desk more than necessary, but that was to be expected, that's just John. In all of the years I've known him he's always thought he's God's gift to women. Don't get me wrong, he's in great shape and not a bad looking guy, but so are many others. He separated from his wife about two months ago and there's been no stopping him since. He must be going through some kind of midlife crisis.

Today is Friday and I'm finishing up with my last client of the day. It's a divorce case and even after I've been doing this for many years, it's still tough to listen to someone's entire life in a nutshell. Of course, I don't need to know all of the details but some clients choose to share. I believe it's to justify it to themselves. I've never been in that kind of situation so I'm sure it isn't simply a walk in the park. This case is particularly difficult and I know it will be weighing on me all weekend.

Once the client leaves I begin packing my briefcase when I hear a soft knock on my door. I look up and see Shelby standing in the doorway.

"Mr. Steele," she says with a smile. "Just dropping off Monday's files."

"Thank you, Shelby. I think I may just take them home with me."

"Would you like me to place them in a bag for you?" she asks.

"No thank you, I think I can fit them in my briefcase," I say and she walks towards me, handing them over. After about three attempts I finally get it to close, maybe I should have taken her up on the bag.

"That was close," she giggles, making me chuckle a bit.

"Well, maybe it's time for a new briefcase. This one has lived past its life expectancy," I say, feeling stupid on how that came out. "Are you ready for the weekend?"

"I am," she replies. "I am babysitting my niece tomorrow night and I think my boyfriend and I will check out that new market on Sunday. It's close to the office."

"My son just went there last weekend. He said it has a *'hipster'* vibe. I'm not exactly sure what he meant by that but he seemed to have a good time."

"Well, this would be our first time going. I'm sure I won't be buying anything, I never do. It's just fun to browse and see all of the interesting things people come up with," she explains. "Is there anything you need before I head out?"

"I think I'm good to go, thank you Shelby," I say and she gives me a big smile.

"Well I hope you have a wonderful weekend Mr. Steele."

"You as well."

As soon as I pull up to the house I'm surprised to see David's car in the driveway. Unlocking the front door, I can already hear Jackson screaming from the living room.

"Hey Dad," David says as I walk into the room.

"Hi Son, it's great to see you. Are you two joining us for dinner?" I ask and right then, Michelle walks in.

"No, he has a date so Jackson will be spending the night with us," she says, wiping her hands on a towel.

I walk up to Michelle, giving her a kiss to say hello. Jackson just realized that I am here and immediately runs to me. Picking him up, I give him a big hug and soon after, he wiggles to get back down to play with his toys.

"Yeah I'm sorry this is so last minute but I have a really good feeling about this girl. She's been working with me for a while and she actually asked me to dinner," David explains. "Speaking of dinner, I need to get going if I don't want to show up late. We are meeting at that Sushi place on 5th."

"That wouldn't make a good first impression, you better get going then," I say and David kisses Jackson goodbye.

Once we sit down for dinner, Michelle tells me about her day and her run in with our neighbor Betty.

"Well, Betty's birthday is on Sunday and she asked if we would stop by for a few hours. A few of the other neighbors are going as well," Michelle begins. "To be honest, I really don't want to go but feel obligated."

"I know what you mean," I sigh. "Well, whenever we want to leave we can just use my cat allergy excuse."

It's an excuse we've used a time or two even though it's a complete lie. Betty has a total of eight cats and there is no surface in her house that is free of cat hair. I love animals but that is just more than I can handle.

"So you're not meeting the girls for coffee tonight?" I ask and Michelle explains that she just didn't feel like going anywhere.

To my surprise, Michelle gets Jackson down for bed quite easy, it's usually always a struggle. Once she comes back downstairs, she places the baby monitor on the side table and suggests that we watch a movie. I'm taken aback by that, I can't recall when we last watched a movie together. Our interests are so different, I'm into horror and she's into chick flicks. Scrolling through the selections on the TV we settle on a romantic drama and I'm sure I will doze off within thirty minutes. Michelle is completely lost in the movie and I'm having a difficult time getting into it. It's not bad at all but my mind seems to be somewhere else. Maybe I'm just tired, it's been a hell of a week.

I get up and walk into the kitchen to get a glass of water. My phone sounds and I pull it out of my back pocket. I notice that the message is from Shelby and I wonder why she would be messaging me. Swiping to the right the

17

message opens and reads *Mr. Steele, I am so sorry to bother you but I left my wallet in the office. Is there any way you would be able to meet me there tomorrow?*

Replying back, I tell her that I can meet her at 10 am. My office is about thirty minutes away from our house but I don't have plans anyway. Returning to the living room I set my glass on the coffee table.

"Hey Michelle, I have to go into the office tomorrow. Our secretary left her wallet by accident. Did you want to come along? We could go out to brunch?"

"What time?"

"I will be leaving here at 9:30 am," I say.

"Well, I'm not sure what time Jackson is getting picked up," she replies.

"Oh, that's right, I completely forgot he was here."

"While you're out that way though, can you pick up a gift card for Betty's party? Oh, and a card?" Michelle asks, yawning just a bit.

"Of course? Any specific place?" I ask, having no idea what Betty likes.

"I don't know, maybe the home décor store or just a restaurant."

"How about a voucher to the shelter for another cat?" I joke, laughing a bit.

"You are so bad Vince," Michelle says, nudging me with her hand.

"Yeah, that wasn't very nice."

"We could just show up with a cat," Michelle jokes.

"Now there's an idea," I reply, chuckling.

The next morning, I arrive at the office right on time and I see Shelby get out of the passenger seat of her car. A man is driving and I'm guessing that he must be her boyfriend. A few seconds later he gets out as well and Shelby introduces us. Just as I suspected, he is her boyfriend. Impression wise, I was definitely not impressed to say the least. He comes across as an arrogant, vain, pretentious fool that spends more time preening himself in the mirror than paying attention to his beautiful girlfriend. Well, it's none of my concern, I'm just happy my sons didn't turn out that way. After retrieving her wallet, Shelby thanks me and I make my way to the store to pick up the gift card. Standing in front of the carrousel of cards near the register, I go for a card that will give her a choice between five different restaurants, safest choice in my opinion.

As I walk into the house I'm met by David with Jackson on his arm. It looks as if they are about to head out.

"Hey David, how was your date?" I ask and he tilts his head back. "Oh, that bad huh?"

"Well, I have never been so bored on a date in my entire life. Safe to say we aren't going out again," he replies.

"Well, I told David that there is no rush in dating anyone anyway. His focus should be on Jackson," Michelle chimes in.

"Yeah I know Mom, it is. I can't be single forever though. Anyway, thanks for taking care of him. I owe you guys big time," David says before heading out of the door.

I walk toward the kitchen, setting the small shopping bag, containing the gift and birthday card on the counter.

"Well, at least Jackson hasn't met this one yet," Michelle says, grabbing some lemonade out of the refrigerator.

"Oh Michelle," I begin. "Sometimes you are just a little bit too hard on him."

"Well, this is what, girl number five he's gone out with in the last six months? Jackson has already met three of them. He is going to confuse that child. Between that and Noelle, I'm not sure Jackson has much of a chance," Michelle vents.

"Hey, you don't mean that. Yes, I agree he should be more selective when introducing people into Jackson's life, I'll talk with him about that," I begin. "Just because he and Noelle didn't work out doesn't make her a terrible mother."

"I know," Michelle sighs. "You're right Vince. Please do talk with him though, will you?"

"Of course," I reply kissing her forehead.

A little backstory on David and Noelle. I knew it was going to be a disaster from the day we met her. She was very possessive over him from the start. David thought it was sweet but learned that after a while it was pure insanity. The moment he decided he wanted out she had a surprise, she was pregnant with Jackson. He tried his best to make it work but they ended their relationship when Jackson turned eighteen months old. Even though their relationship was turbulent I think Noelle is a great mother. She is very loving and attentive and Jackson is a very happy little boy. She actually keeps in touch with us, sending us pictures here and there. I've never quite figured out why Michelle despises her so much.

The next few months pass and it's already mid-October. The office has been very busy, which is great. Running a small firm can prove difficult at times, especially with all of the big-name cooperation's around. Luckily, our customers are very loyal and through their word of mouth plus advertisements, we've never experienced hard times thus far.

We've all gotten to know Shelby much better as well and she has really become part of the team. She's very outgoing and bubbly. Her work ethic is excellent and she's been surprising us all with baked treats every Friday. I guess baking is one of her hobbies and she is very good at it. There's been a time or two where things slowed down and I found myself seeking a conversation with her. I've learned that she's been with her boyfriend for a few years now and from a few little remarks my first impression of him was spot on. I wonder why she puts up with him, she's absolutely gorgeous with a wonderful personality. Total package if you ask me.

Chapter Three

Vincent

God, it's been such a long day. It's already 5:30 pm and I'm just now shutting down the computer. Grabbing my jacket and briefcase, I turn off the light to my office before heading toward the front door. After locking up, I make my way down the steps and notice Shelby sitting on a bench outside. I remember her leaving about thirty minutes ago and I wonder why she is still here, maybe she's waiting for someone. I did overhear that her car was at the mechanics.

"Shelby, what are you still doing here?"

"Long story," she replies with a half-smile.

"Well, I have time," I counter and now we have a full smile.

"My car is in the shop and my *'original'* ride was unable to make it."

"I can give you a lift, it's no problem at all," I offer and her eyes widen in surprise.

"Oh, thank you so much, but I don't want to inconvenience you. Besides, my sister will be coming to pick me up."

"Is your sister already on her way?"

"No, she gets off in about thirty minutes," she says and I shake my head.

"You've already been sitting out here for a while. Come on, just message her and let her know you've found a ride."

For a moment, I see hesitation written all over her face, maybe I shouldn't have been so forward.

"Only if it really isn't a bother?" she asks, her eyes studying me.

"Not at all," I reply.

She follows me to my car and I open the passenger door for her. The look on her face can be described as a total surprise.

"Thank you," she says as she gets in.

"My pleasure," I respond with a smile, shutting the door.

I walk around to the other side and get in. Once I start the car, I ask Shelby to enter her address into the built-in navigation system. There's an awkward silence between us for a few minutes and suddenly curiosity has gotten the better of me.

"Shelby, may I ask a question?" I begin. "And if you'd rather not answer it's completely fine."

"Oh boy," she giggles. "Sure."

"Your 'original' ride, it was your boyfriend, correct?" I regret it as soon as it leaves my lips. I know it isn't any of my business. I hope I haven't overstepped. Glancing over I see her wearing a tiny smile, looking down.

"How did you know?"

"Just a wild guess," I reply.

"Yeah, I'm not sure why I trusted him to be here. It's not like I can ever rely on him anyway."

"May I speak freely?"

"Yes, of course," she says, looking over at me.

"I know we've only worked together for about three months but I think you are an amazing young woman. Don't let anyone take advantage of you. To be quite honest, I think you deserve better," I explain and if my imagination isn't fooling me I could have sworn I just saw her blush a little.

Her boyfriend has been to the office on three separate occasions and every time I've seen him he comes across as a charismatic prick. I can see the attraction, he is a very good-looking man, but he knows it as well. As we sit in rush-hour traffic, I am not one bit aggravated. I normally detest traffic jams but the conversation between Shelby and I has been nothing short of wonderful. She makes it so easy and I find myself sharing a few things about my private life, which takes me by surprise. Normally I keep those things to myself, but she seems genuinely interested in what I have to say and I feel as if I can trust her, even if it sounds crazy. I haven't smiled this much in years, it really feels nice. Once I pull up to her apartment, she gives me another smile before unbuckling her seatbelt.

"Mr. Steele, thank you so much for taking me home, I really appreciate it," she says, her lips still wearing a smile. By the way, she has the most beautiful lips I have ever seen in my entire life.

"I'm happy that I was able to help. Oh, and Shelby, when we are outside of work you can call me Vince."

"Does that mean I will have the pleasure of seeing you outside of work again?"

That statement left me speechless. It wasn't so much what she said, it was how she said it. That little smirk, along with that look in her eye.

"Goodnight Vincent.".

"Goodnight Shelby," I reply.

As I drive away I try to decipher what just happened. Was she flirting with me? No, a woman like her wouldn't in the least bit be interested in someone like me. I could be her father. Well, not really, I would have had to start quite young for that. In any case, she's thirty-four and I'm turning fifty. Who knows, maybe she likes older men. Well, there's nothing wrong with a little flirtation anyway.

Shelby

I must be out of my mind flirting with my boss like that. What the hell got into me? I don't know him very well but there is a sadness that radiates off him. He is very different from all of the other men in the office. He's quiet, very polite and almost a little intimidating. I'm sure it has something to do with his age. He's probably close to fifteen years older than me but there is something so intriguing about him. For his age, his dark-blonde hair only reveals a few stray greys. That actually even makes him more attractive in my opinion. I've seen him steal a few glances out of the corner of my eye. In the moments I actually do make eye contact with him, he comes across as a little boy who just got caught. I love it. Today was the first day I really got to look into those gorgeous blue eyes, and they are absolutely beautiful. I could literally stare into them the rest of my life and get lost.

When I walk up to the door of my apartment I am immediately ripped from my daydream from the music blasting from inside. Probably a good thing since it's not appropriate to lust after my boss, even if he weren't married. As I walk inside, Chad is passed out on the couch. I should have known better than to trust him to be there for me. Judging from the empty bottle of whiskey along with several empty beer bottles it looks as though it was just another typical day for him. It wasn't always like this. There was a time when we were happy and in love. About four months ago he walked out of his job and hasn't found it necessary to find a new one. I suppose there is no incentive on going out to find another since I am paying all the bills anyway. Chad comes from a very wealthy family and his mother has been providing him with 'spending money' since he's been unemployed. Unfortunately, instead of helping me with the bills, it's used for whatever he wants, mainly alcohol. Sometimes I ask myself if I am an idiot. He seems pretty content just mooching off me. We've been together for three years now so the idea of walking away terrifies me a bit. I hate being alone, I was alone for many years before meeting Chad. Then again, that little talk with Vincent may have just given me the courage I need to make a change. I very well may just be wasting my time. I've voiced my concerns to Chad so many times and seeing him passed out on the couch yet again is sending me into a rage. Obviously, I am not taken seriously in this relationship. I may just be better off on my own.

I walk over to the stereo and turn it off, cleaning up the living room and discarding the alcohol bottles. I would love nothing more than to wake him up and tell him I am done with this behavior, but with him in this condition I won't be getting much of a response, nor would he remember it in the morning. I decide to just go on like usual and ignore the situation. After eating some leftovers, I take a shower and crawl into bed with my tablet. It's not late but the sight of Chad wasted on the couch is one I don't care to see.

Chapter Four

Vincent

It's Saturday night and I haven't been able to get Shelby out of my head since dropping her off at the apartment yesterday. Not only is she gorgeous but she seems to bring a smile to my face when I just think of her. I'm delusional. Even if I were younger and single, she and I would have never crossed paths in life. We are very different, maybe that is the attraction.

"Vince!" I hear Michelle yelling from the kitchen. "Are you deaf? Get the door, I have my hands full right now."

Swiftly getting up from the sofa I hurry toward the front door. Shelby completely consumed my thoughts. I must admit, it was nice to escape, even for just a few minutes.

"Hey Dad, thought you were gonna let us freeze out here," Luke comments and I lean in to give him a hug.

"Where's Ashley?" I ask when I see that it's only him and Libby.

"Oh, she had to run by her parents to help them take care of a few things for her grandmother's birthday party next weekend. I'm so glad I'm not there, I would be bored out of my mind."

"Well, it's a big one, right? Isn't she turning eighty?" I ask after they step inside.

"Yes, the big eight zero. The poor woman doesn't even want a party, but I suppose she has nothing to say in the matter."

"Well, we all know Ashley's mom loves a party," I comment, remembering Luke and Ashley's wedding. "Alright, we just have to wait for David, I'm sure he'll be here any moment."

"Oh, David wanted me to tell you he can't make it tonight. He has a date," Luke informs me and I raise my eyebrow.

"A date? Doesn't he have Jackson this weekend?" I ask.

"He traded weekends with Noelle. I guess they are on good terms right now," Luke replies, as we sit at the dining table. I did have that little talk with David about introducing people into Jackson's life and I hope he took it to heart.

At dinner, Libby and I play our favorite game of *'Who is the first to make a happy plate'*. Of course, I always let her win and seeing her face light up as she holds up her cleared plate sends pure happiness straight to my heart. Michelle doesn't like this game at all and thinks I coddle her too much. That's where Michelle and I are very different. She isn't very grandmotherly to the grandkids. Sure, she loves them dearly but she treats them like they are little adults. She won't get down on the floor to play with them, or make a fool out of herself. She would rather just read them a book or tell them to play with each other. To each their own I guess. I remember when Luke and Ashely announced they were pregnant with Libby my wife wasn't overjoyed. Later she told me she was just too young to be a grandmother. I thought she was out of her mind. Michelle has always been very concerned with outward appearances. That is the main reason we live in this monstrosity of a house, to show others that we are made of money. I have no idea why we ever needed six bedrooms.

Once Michelle and I clear all of the dishes we retreat into the family room and within minutes, Libby has transformed it into a playroom. She is the spitting image of Luke, looks and personality. Watching her play brings back memories of the boys when they were young. I really miss those times. I regret that I missed out on bits and pieces of their lives. I am grateful that Michelle videotaped every soccer, baseball and football game that I wasn't able to attend. God, I'm sitting here reflecting on the past as if my life is over, I'm not that old.

Once Luke and Libby leave, I decide it's time to turn in for the night. Michelle is already upstairs and I set the alarm before heading up myself. As I walk into the bedroom, she is sitting in bed looking at a magazine. I almost feel as if I share my bed with a stranger. The last time we had sex was about six months ago and it felt as if she was doing me a favor, or it was her obligatory duty. To the outside we are this happy go lucky couple with a perfect life. On the inside I'm slowly falling apart. I miss the touch of another human being, I miss feeling wanted and loved.

"Vince, did you set the alarm?" Michelle asks as I remove my pants and shirt, laying them over the chair.

"I did," I reply and she gives me a little smile.

"I was reading this interesting article about a woman that is involved in a polygamous relationship," she begins. "That entire lifestyle is so strange to me."

"I agree," I say, getting into bed, wondering if I'm about to get turned down again. Hell, it's worth a shot.

I move closer, moving her hair behind her ear. My lips make their way to her cheek, planting kisses down her neck.

"Vince, what are you doing?" she asks and I just continue. "Vince, I'd really like to finish my magazine. Can we do this another time?"

"Of course, sweetheart," I reply, backing away. It's no use to get angry. It wouldn't accomplish anything anyway.

Switching off the lamp on my nightstand, I turn on my side, facing the window just staring into nothing. A few seconds later, a grin graces my face – *'Does that mean I will have the pleasure of seeing you outside of work again?'* – the sentence that left me speechless. The mere thought of Shelby makes my heart race, a feeling I haven't had in years. The way my name rolled off her tongue sent chills down my spine, I'd give anything to hear it again.

The next day I take on the dreaded task of raking the leaves in our yard. We have many northern red oak trees on our property and even though they are beautiful to look at, the cleanup is time consuming. About an hour and eight yard bags later I'm finally finished and starving. Removing my shoes before walking inside, I'm met by Michelle in the family room.

"What do you say we go out for lunch today?" she suggests and I think it sounds like a wonderful idea.

While in the car we throw around a few ideas and decide on the Seafood Market. It's a fairly small restaurant with the best seafood around. We've been there quite a few times and have never been disappointed. Even though we are in a big city, when dining there, it gives you a small-town feeling. Pulling into the parking lot, they don't seem to be very busy. At dinner, parking becomes a challenge and there have been numerous times that we've had to park across the street. As soon as we walk in we are greeted by the usual hostess and she seats us at a table near the bar, informing us that our waiter will be with us momentarily. We each grab a menu from the little stand on the table and browse the selections. The menu changes every month so it's a surprise every time. After ordering our food, Michelle mentions that her sister called earlier this morning. As she continues talking, my attention is drawn to a voice I recognize. Looking up to see if my suspicion is correct, I spot Shelby standing at the bar, talking to another woman. I've only ever seen her in her work attire and all I can say is she looks amazing in jeans. She's wearing her hair in waves and it reaches the small of her back. She usually has it pinned up at work and I had no idea it was that long. It's beautiful, just like her. For a moment I wonder if I should say hello and introduce my wife, I suppose that would be the right thing to do. A few seconds later she says goodbye to the woman behind the bar, well I guess she made the decision for me.

"Hey Michelle, what do you say we stop by my parents house on the way home. We haven't been for a visit in a while," I say and at that moment, our food arrives.

"How long of a visit are we talking?" she asks, huffing a bit.

"I swear I won't make it an afternoon thing, thirty minutes tops," I reply and I can tell she's thinking about it.

"Vince, I really have a lot of things to get together for the community meeting next week. Plus, I have to go over the training binder for work. How about you drop me off at home and visit with them?"

On second thought, I think that's a better idea anyway. Even though my wife and parents get along fine, they don't always see eye to eye on things. For example, my mom was never able to understand why Michelle chose to work instead of staying home to raise the boys. She never said a word to her but I've heard it several times.

After dropping Michelle at home, I make my way to Brooklyn. Believe it or not, my parents still live in the same townhouse that we were raised in, mom just didn't want to move. I would love to have them a bit closer to me but hell would have to freeze over before that would happen. My sisters live close by so they check in on them here and there. Parking my car in front of their house I make my way up the steps, ringing the doorbell.

"Vincent! What a surprise!" my mom says pulling me in for a big squeeze. She is one little lady but definitely has a grip on her.

"Hey mom, just stopping by to say hello. Is dad home?" I ask, removing my coat and hanging it on the coatrack in the hall.

"Yes, he is in the living room. Would you like some coffee Vincent?"

"Sure, that sounds good," I reply, bending down and kissing her cheek.

Heading into the living room, I see my dad sitting on the sofa, watching TV. He immediately presses the mute button and begins to tell me about the new woman in my brother Rob's life. Mom joins us about ten minutes later, holding a tray with three coffee cups and condiments. I get up to grab the tray, setting it on the coffee table for her.

"Vincent, where is Michelle?" mom asks and I knew that was going to come.

"She has a few things to take care of concerning work and the community meeting next week. She told me to say hello though."

After about fifteen minutes of conversation I see my dad grabbing my mom's hand, kissing it and mom turns to him, giving him a big smile. That is exactly what I am talking about. They have been together for so long and they still have it. Where did I go wrong?

"Vincent, is everything alright? You look lost in thought," mom asks, with a hint of concern in her voice.

"I'm okay. How are you still so happy after being together so many years?"

"Are things not good at home?" mom asks, her eyes focused on me.

"I don't know. Sometimes I feel as if we are complete strangers just sharing a house. Most of the time I don't feel a connection to her, it saddens me," I confess and mom immediately walks over to sit next to me, grabbing my hand and rubbing it with her other hand.

"Well, she's never been the warm kind," my dad begins. "I never thought the two of you were a very good match. Everything is either black or white for her, no grey areas at all."

"Vincent, I'm sure things will be all right. Dad and I had rough patches as well, you just have to push through. Things will get better, you just have to work on it."

I just have to work on it. I've tried for so many years and things have only gotten worse. I never shared that Michelle and I went to counseling, nor the lack of intimacy, I just keep all of it to myself.

It's Monday morning and I am looking forward to seeing Shelby at work. I couldn't get her off of my mind all weekend, it's the only thing that brought a smile to my face. Thinking about it right now, it sounds very pathetic actually, but a little fantasizing never hurt anyone though, right?

Shelby

What a weekend I've had. One of the most productive ones in a long time. After wasting my breath, pleading Chad to make a change I finally realized, it's never going to happen. I don't know what got into me but I told him to get the hell out of my apartment. To my surprise, he did, grabbing just about all of his belongings aside from furniture. I must admit, I cried my eyes out that first night by myself, but last night was much better. I feel as if I can finally breathe and I feel free.

Walking into the office I'm greeted by John who shoots me a big smile and a wink. Ever since I started, John has been very flirtatious and to be honest, it is slowly getting on my last nerve. Even if I were attracted to him I wouldn't start anything with someone I work with, it's just too messy.

After filling the coffee maker with filtered water, I add a couple scoops of coffee into the filter before pressing the brew button. About twenty seconds later the front door opens and I see Vincent walk in.

"Good morning Mr. Steele," I begin. "Did you have a good weekend?"

"Good morning Shelby. It was uneventful," he replies. "How was yours? Did you get your car back?"

"I did, running good as new," I reply. "I know I sound like a broken record but thank you again for the ride and advice you gave me as well."

"Oh, you're very welcome. I wasn't sure if I was a bit too forward, meddling in your affairs."

"Not at all, you opened my eyes to something that I've been avoiding for months."

"Well, sometimes it's easier to talk to someone who doesn't have any involvement," he says and he's completely right.

"In any case, thank you," I smile. "I'll have your coffee ready in just a few minutes.

As soon as the coffee is ready, I pour a cup and walk into Vincent's office. Standing in the doorway, I stop and just take him in, completely engrossed in a file. He has a court appearance today so I'm sure he's preparing. He had to have felt me standing there because a second later our eyes meet and a little smile comes over his lips.

"Oh great, thank you Shelby," he begins and I walk over to his desk, handing the cup to him. "I definitely need that this morning. I'm not very confident about this case."

"I'm sure you will do fine. By the way, I love that tie," I comment…oh my god, why did I say that? I do have a weakness for ties, especially striped ones.

"Thank Shelby, it's my lucky one. My wife absolutely hates it," he replies, with a bit of a chuckle. He doesn't smile often, but when he does, it's beautiful.

"Well, you wear it very well," I reply. "Blue looks really good on you."

I stand there for a few more minutes and we chit chat back and forth until we are interrupted by the phone ringing on my desk. I hurry out the door to take the call. Wrong number but it was time to get out of that office anyway. The more I talk to Vincent, the more I like him. He has quite a few years on me but damn, he is a sight for sore eyes, too bad he is married.

About two hours later, the front door opens and a young man comes walking in. He must be in his twenties and has a killer smile.

"Good morning," I say standing up. "How can I help you?"

"Hey, I'm looking for my dad, is he in his office?" the young man replies.

"Who is your dad?" I ask, trying to place his face to one of the men here in the office.

"Oh sorry, Vince Steele," he responds with another smile and I do notice a little bit of a resemblance. His hair is just a little darker and he's got green eyes, otherwise, I could see this being a young Vincent.

"He has an appointment at court today and I'm estimating him to be back in about an hour. Is it something urgent? Would you like me to call him?" I ask and he shakes his head.

"Nah, I was just in this part of town and thought I would stop by. You must be the new secretary. What's your name?" he asks in quite the flirtatious tone.

38

"Shelby Hunter, pleased to meet you," I smile and two seconds later, his cell phone rings.

"Damn, I have to take this," he says as he looks at the screen. "It was great to meet you. I'm sure I'll see you again."

With that, he is out the door and John comes walking up to my desk.

"That must have been David," John snickers. "He definitely took a liking to you."

"Oh, I don't think so, he was just here looking for Mr. Steele," I reply, scrunching my forehead.

"Well, he's a nice kid. A little on the wild side but good overall. He has a son that just turned two recently," John explains. "Wow, look at me laying it all out there, I'm sure Vince wouldn't appreciate that. He's more of the private type."

"I've gathered as much," I reply, grabbing a file out of my desk drawer. "Well, I better get back to work."

"Oh yeah of course. I'll be in my office," he replies before walking away.

There is something about John that totally creeps me out, I'm not sure what it is though. He's fairly decent looking but he has this thing about him that just screams dirty old man. Sends shivers down my spine, and not in a good way.

After finishing with the file, I walk into Vincent's office to place it on his desk. To the right there is a tall book case and a photograph catches my eye. Whenever I come in here I don't usually look around so that's probably why I hadn't noticed it before. Walking toward it, I pick it up to study it. I recognize his son in the picture and this must be the rest of the family. Wow, his other son is the spitting image of him, right down to the smile. This must be Mrs. Steele. I pictured her just a bit different. She seems fairly plain, dark blonde hair with the typical short haircut that every woman past forty seems to get. Suddenly I'm startled by Vincent's voice.

"Hello Shelby," he greets me as he places his briefcase on the desk.

"Oh sorry," I begin, how I am supposed to explain why I am holding his family picture in my hands? "I came in to drop off a file and I noticed your picture."

He walks over to me, standing fairly close, which throws me a bit, he usually keeps his distance.

"We took that a few years ago in Italy. It was a really good trip," he replies and seems as if he is reminiscing.

"You're not Italian, are you?" I ask. Obviously, there is nothing Italian about his last name but he does have a bit of a different look.

"I'm not," he replies. "I'm actually part Ukrainian."

"Oh wow, really? Do you speak it?" I ask, hopefully I'm not digging too much.

"Just a little here and there. Not enough to get around in the Ukraine though."

"How long have you been married?" I ask out of curiosity, placing the picture back on the shelf

"Twenty-six years," he replies and my eyes widen.

"That is quite commendable, amazing," I counter and he takes a deep breath.

"We make it work. Marriage isn't always easy," he replies and there is a hint of sadness in his eye. Seems as if there is more to the story.

"By the way, how did court go?" I ask and our eyes meet.

"Wonderful. We won," he grins.

"Well, looks as if you wore the right tie then," I giggle, sending another big smile to his face.

Chapter Five

Vincent

I absolutely love talking to Shelby. I'm usually very private when it comes to my personal life but with her I seem to open up more than I have with anyone before. She told me that David stopped by the office earlier and I really wish I hadn't missed him. It's rare that any members of my family come by for a visit. Sitting at my desk I stare out of the window, why couldn't I have met someone like Shelby when I was younger?

Over the week I have gotten to know her a bit better as well. She isn't originally from New York. She was born in Southern California and moved around a lot as a child. She shared that her father had a hard time holding a job and they would end up bouncing from state to state before settling in New York when she was seventeen. That is a life I definitely cannot relate to, I've always had stability…some call that boring but I've always been very comfortable with it.

Now that I have a reason to look forward to going to work, the week always flies by in an instant. I feel as if I blinked and it's already Friday. Finishing up a few last things on the computer, I am interrupted by Shelby knocking on the doorframe. It's an interruption I welcome any day.

"Mr. Steele. I am heading out, is there anything else that you need?" she asks with a warm smile, and my thoughts immediately shift to the inappropriate side.

I must have quite the smirk on my face because she counters her own question with a *What?*

"Oh nothing," I reply. "Was just thinking of something."

"I'd love to get into that head of yours one day, I'm sure it would be quite interesting," she replies with a wink. "Have a great weekend Mr. Steele."

"You too Shelby," I reply.

Okay, right about now you're probably thinking Whoa, when did they get so friendly with each other? I honestly don't have the answer, it just happened. The playful back and forth banter is always the best part of my day. A little flirting back and forth never hurt anyone. To be quite honest, it's actually improved my home life as well. The lack of intimacy doesn't seem to bother me anymore. I suppose I found something to keep my mind off of the issues that used to consume me. Like I said, it's harmless…it's just words.

It's Saturday evening and Michelle just put the lasagna on the table. Luke, Ashley and Libby are at Ashley's grandmother's birthday party so today we're joined by David and Jackson. About halfway through the meal the conversation takes a turn when David brings up Shelby's name.

"Dad, your new secretary is hot as hell," he exclaims and Michelle takes a deep breath.

"Language David," she growls.

"Sorry mom," David apologizes. "But seriously, I thought about asking for her phone number."

"I think she may be a little old for you David," I reply. How awkward would that be? Her and I flirting during the week and my son wanting to take her out on the weekend.

"I don't discriminate," he laughs and suddenly Michelle has become interested.

"Vince, how old is she?"

"Thirty-four," I reply, wiping my mouth with the napkin.

"Why do you think that is too old for him?" Michelle asks, looking at me.

"Well, it's a ten-year gap. It's proven that women are ahead of men where age is concerned anyway. Just not sure if they would have a lot in common."

"So, do you know her pretty well then?" Michelle asks and I wonder where she is going with this.

"All I know is that she is a great secretary and keeps the office on track. What she does in her personal time is not my concern," I reply. "With that being said, if you'd like to ask for her number, that is fine. As long as you don't cost me an employee."

After that sentence the conversation switched to something a little on the lighter side. I found that I got quite defensive where Shelby was concerned. Telling my son that a ten-year age gap may be too much but, in the meantime, I have fifteen years on her. Then again, I'm not asking for her phone number nor am I trying to date her.

That night as we get ready for bed Michelle gives me a few strange glances.

"What?" I ask, as I climb into bed.

"Don't you think it's a little cliché?"

"What are you talking about?"

"Oh, come on Vince. Hiring a young, hot secretary that you all can gawk at and fantasize over. I'm sure it wasn't her qualifications that made the cut," she continues and I'm actually quite surprised how catty she is getting.

"Why are you judging someone you've never even met? Where is this coming from?" I ask and she shoots me a deadly look.

"Why are you defending her?"

"Alright, I'm done discussing this. It is ridiculous to be quite honest. I didn't hire her, John did. If you are displeased you can speak to him about it."

Well, that shut her up quickly. I know it was my tone. I'm usually very even-tempered but her attitude was just so juvenile.

The next morning Michelle apologizes for her stint last night, saying she wasn't feeling well. That's a first, the words *I'm sorry* never come easy for her, but she probably realized that she was in the wrong.

"Hey Vince, Miranda asked if we'd like to join them for dinner tonight, what do you think?" Michelle asks.

"Sounds like a great idea, where did they want to meet?" I ask, knowing it will probably be the Thai place about two blocks from their house.

"Thai Temple," she responds and I grin.

Miranda and Phil took one trip to Thailand about four years ago and have since been hooked on Asian cuisine. I'm fairly open and adventurous when it comes to different foods, so is Michelle. In that regard we have always meshed very well.

Right now, Michelle is completely engrossed in a new romance novel so I retreat into my study. I brought some work home with me on Friday and I figure I could get a little head start. Opening the first file I find little sticky notes left by Shelby. This is the first time that I've actually missed seeing her face. Looking at my phone sitting next to the lamp on my desk I'm so tempted to send her a message, but what would I say? I supposed I could thank her for reviewing my charts for me. Yes, that is exactly what I will do. Scrolling through my contacts I select her name and start typing. *Shelby, I hope you're having a great weekend. Just wanted to thank you for the hard work you put in and making my life easier with those sticky notes.*

I set my phone back on the desk and start to work. A few minutes later, I receive a message notification. Swiping to the right, I see the message is from Shelby and it reads, *Who is this?* For a moment I gasp, maybe she does this for everyone at the office. I think for a moment and then reply,

It's Vince…don't tell me everyone gets this special treatment…jk.

I don't even have time to set the phone down before the next message appears. *Oh, hi Vincent. Actually, I do…but yours are the only ones with the smiley faces.* Reading that message puts a smile on my face and I place my phone back on the desk. That wasn't so hard.

Shelby

I was very surprised to receive a text message from
Vincent. Totally came out of nowhere. At first, he was so
closed up and almost unapproachable but ever since he
gave me that ride home, things have become more relaxed.
Maybe that was the icebreaker. He smiles a lot more too
now and I love our little flirtatious conversations. I
definitely need to watch it though, I can totally see myself
falling for this guy, but he belongs to someone else. Damn
it, just my luck. Well, he's way to old me for anyway...but
so handsome and charming.

Breaking off my relationship with Chad is the best thing I
could have ever done. It took a little time to get used to
being on my own, but not having a bum lying on my
couch messing up the entire apartment has been such a
breath of fresh air. He and his brother stopped by here
Friday night to pick up the rest of his belongings which
consisted of a bed, nightstand and dresser that were in the
spare bedroom. Well, now that chapter of my life has
closed. Time for the next one to begin.

My sister Kristi should be here in a few minutes. She is two
years older than me, married and has a little girl named
Hayley that I absolutely adore. Hayley is pretty much my
surrogate daughter. She just turned ten last month and is a
real little lady. Toy stores are so yesterday, she's into
jewelry now...her words. I prepared homemade pizza for
tonight and just put it in the oven as my doorbell rings.

"It's open Kristi," I yell from the kitchen and I hear the door open and shut.

"Shelby, how many times have I told you to keep your door locked? We don't live in the Midwest," Kristi says as she greets me in the kitchen.

"I swear, I just unlocked it a few minutes ago," I say, giving her a big smile.

"You're such a bad liar," Kristi and I chuckles and I start to laugh.

"Hey, where's Hayley?"

"She got invited to a last-minute sleepover so I dropped her off on the way here," Kristi explains and I suppose I could have loaded the pizza with veggies had I known, now we're stuck with plain cheese. Once the pizza is done, we sit on the couch and catch up. As I talk about my job and the people I work with, she gives me a peculiar look.

"So, who is this Vincent," Kristi inquires.

"Oh, he's my boss. Well, one of them. John is the other boss," I explain and her eyes get a little bigger.

"You openly flirt with your boss like that?" she asks, looking surprised.

"Well, not in front of everyone, it's more just like a back and forth between us," I say.

"So how old is this Vincent?"

"I think he's fifty."

"Fifty?! Shelby, why on earth are you flirting around with some guy that's close to dad's age. That's weird," she says, scrunching her forehead.

"Kristi, come on. We're just playing around. He's married anyway. By the way, Dad is Fifty-Seven."

"Oh god," she says, resting her forehead in her hands. "What am I going to do with you?"

"Don't worry about me, I'm not fifteen years old."

"That's exactly why I'm worried, if you were fifteen I would blame it on not being rational. There's a fine line between fun and when things turn toward a direction you didn't intend. Just be careful Shelby."

"Okay, I will," I reply, rolling my eyes.

I suppose she's worried because my choice in men has been quite questionable over the years. I don't blame her, I know how to pick them for sure.

I change the subject to upcoming plans for thanksgiving next month. We used to celebrate at my parents house but they've been switching off with Kristi when it comes to the festivities. My brother, Matt will be home on leave from North Dakota. Matt is the baby of the family and has been in the military for the last seven years. His birthday falls on thanksgiving this year and he will be twenty-seven. I haven't seen him in about a year so I am very excited.

Kristi ends up staying for a few hours and it was really fun having a girl's night. We've always been very close and she's been my rock during low points in my life. I don't know what I would do without her. After she leaves, I go into the kitchen and grab a bottle of wine. Removing the cork, I pour about half a glass for and return to the couch, turning on the TV. Grabbing my phone off the armrest I position it and snap a picture of my wine glass on the table. I was about to post it on my social media account but instead, decide to send it to Vincent along with the following message *Soooo I may or may not make it into work tomorrow.....just kidding. A little Moscato before bed never hurt anyone right?*

When I don't get a message back I regret sending the text. We're friendly with each other but I may have gone a bit too far. Finishing off my glass I jump into the shower. After drying my hair and slipping into my shorts and t-shirt I walk over to the couch to retrieve my phone so I can charge it and notice I have a message waiting for me. I see it's from Vincent and it makes me smile instantly. *I sure do hope you will make it to work tomorrow, seeing you is the highlight of my day.* Oh my god! I didn't think my smile could get any bigger but it did. I never would have expected for him to say that. Maybe he's had some wine tonight as well. After replying with a wink, I head into my bedroom to go to sleep. I end up tossing and turning for what seems like hours. Unhooking my phone from the charging cable I open the message app and stare at the last message Vincent sent me. For a moment, I imagine those beautiful pale blue eyes staring directly at me, saying those exact words before his lip rides up in a little smirk…keep your distance Shelby, keep your distance.

Chapter Six

Vincent

That blouse Shelby is wearing today makes my imagination run wild. Having these thoughts at work is definitely not appropriate nor comfortable. All I can say is I'm glad I am sitting behind a desk. I must admit, I haven't felt this alive in years, it's a wonderful feeling and it leaves me longing for more. Longing for something I can't have. She is off limits, actually I am the one off limits here. Time to get my head out of fantasy land and back into my files. I've scheduled a small staff meeting at the end of the day to talk about a few things, including time off during the holiday season. As I am preparing for a case, I notice Shelby walking in, holding a folder.

"Mr. Steele," she begins. I love it when she says my name. "Mr. Preston asked if I could drop this off with you. He was wondering if you had time to look things over to make sure he doesn't have any errors," Shelby relays, handing me a folder.

I smile as I take the folder from her hands. Mr. Preston, better known as Bryce to me, is one of our newer lawyers and I've become his mentor in a sense.

"Of course, thank you Shelby," I say and she turns to walk away. "Shelby?"

"Yes Mr. Steele," she replies turning her head and looking over her shoulder. That is a view I will never forget, I already know it.

"How was the wine last night?"

"Oh," she says with a smile before turning around and walking toward me. "It was alright. I'm usually more of a tequila girl. Wine was all I had though."

"Hopefully it's not like that song," I say, chuckling a bit.

"What song?" she asks with a smile.

"You know, that country song. *TEQUILA MAKES HER CLOTHES FALL OFF*," I counter and I notice her lip ride up in a little smirk.

"Well, Mr. Steele. I suppose you may have to buy me a shot one day to find out," she responds, biting her lip before walking out of my office.

That was intense and right now I am imagining her pencil skirt scrunched at her hips and her straddling me in my chair. I'm sure those lips feel incredible and I wish I could just have one taste. Who am I kidding, one taste would never satisfy me, it would be a tease.

"Hey Vince," John's voice rips me out of my daydream. "I'm back, shall we have the meeting?"

"Yes, of course. Can you lock the front door and gather everyone in the conference room?"

"Sure thing," he replies before walking off. Taking a deep breath, I lean back in my chair, rubbing my temples. Never in my life has a woman driven me this insane or turned me on so suddenly without physical contact. Once I collect myself, I go in the direction of the conference room and see everyone is there. As I speak, I see Shelby taking notes. A few questions arise from my colleagues and I address them.

"So Vince, about the holiday party. Same as last year?" John asks.

"Actually, I'm glad you brought that up. We can definitely go for a small intimate dinner as we do every year. The other option is coming together with a few of the other firms and reserving a ballroom of a hotel. Now, the ticket will be $40 per person but it will include dinner. Jack from Baum and Associates contacted me via email over the weekend, asking if we'd be interested. Take a few days to think on it. I need to give him an answer by Friday," I say and judging from the expression on everyone's face, this may be a winner. I think it's a great idea. More of a formal event, a reason to get dressed up and mingle with some of the other firms. As of right now, Jack says he has ten firms that have signed up for sure.

Wednesday snuck up fast and it's already 4 pm. I just returned from court and unfortunately didn't win this case. I told my client that we should definitely think about filing an appeal. Walking around the office I notice it's unusually quiet. Where is everyone? I see Shelby exiting Bryce's office with a stack of printer paper.

"Hey Shelby, are you the only one here?"

"I am," she replies. "It was so slow that they decided to call it a day."

"Oh, I see. What's that saying? Once the boss is away, the others will play…something along those lines. So why did you stay?"

"Well," she replies, sitting on her desk. "I like to play with the boss."

That comment completely took me by surprise and I feel as if I need to pinch myself. This has got to be my imagination.

"I'm so sorry Vincent," she says giggling. "You set it up so perfectly."

"Playing around with me, huh? I see how it is…and you're still laughing."

"I'm sorry, I totally needed that laugh. I think I'm getting sick and I look and feel like shit."

"You look beautiful," I reply and for a moment you could hear a pin drop in the room. Looking at me she reveals the most beautiful smile I've ever seen.

"Thank you, Vincent. I really appreciate that," she says, sounding sincere. Has no one told her that lately? This last boyfriend she had must have really been a loser.

"You're welcome," I say before pausing a moment. "If a smile like that is the result of my statement, I will tell you that you are beautiful at least once every day."

"Oh wow," she says, her hand covering her face just a bit. "You're making me blush Vincent."

"Good. It makes you even more gorgeous…even though I didn't think that was possible," I smile and she reveals another blush. "Can I ask you a question?"

"Of course," she replies, her eyes full of curiosity.

"Is there a reason you call me Vincent instead of Vince?"

"Oh, do you prefer Vince?"

"No, not really. I was just wondering,"

"Well, yes there is," she begins. "Vincent is such a beautiful name, and I think that shortening it really is a shame."

"Wow, my mother would love you," I say chuckling. "She really dislikes when others call me Vince."

"Well, mom knows best, right?"

We spend the next hour talking. Thankfully we weren't interrupted by a phone or anyone else walking in. I really feel as if we have connected on a deeper level and I truly value this …well, I'm not sure what this is exactly…but I value every minute of it.

On my drive home, I can't get Shelby's beautiful smile out of my head. That witty comment, the way she responds to my words, her laugh…everything about her. How can one person completely turn my life upside down – but in a wonderful way.

Michelle has been unusually happy tonight and she even cooked my favorite meal. I'm kind of wondering what she is up to. The last time she did this she backed into a light pole with the car, completely bashing in the trunk.

"So, honey, how was work today?" she asks as I spoon the salad onto my plate.

"It was fine. I lost a case but I'm confident that with a little more work we will win," I reply and she gives me a warm smile.

"Well, I'm sure you will. You're one of the best lawyers around," she winks and now I know there has got to be something going on.

"Why thank you Michelle," I say. "That is very sweet of you to say. How was your day? What time will the book club ladies be here tonight?"

"Oh, we cancelled this week's get together. A few of them couldn't make it so it really wasn't worth it. We are actually thinking about meeting at a local coffee shop next time," she says and pauses. "Well, speaking of my day, a couple of us girls were thinking about taking a little trip to the Hamptons. Just for about three or four days. I just wanted to run it by you before agreeing."

There it is, I knew there was something she wanted. I'm sure this trip will set us back just a bit and I'm not even talking about the accommodations. When a few of the girls get together, they literally shop until they drop.

"Sure, sounds like a great idea. When were you thinking on going?"

"Next Thursday to Sunday late. I know it's last minute but with work being so busy, getting away will be nice," she replies and I nod, smiling.

Four days on my own, I am actually really looking forward to it. It will be relaxing for sure. I actually may be able to tackle some projects at work after hours that I never seem to have the time for. With no one waiting for me at home, it won't matter when I return. Who knows, this may be exactly what our marriage needs, a little break and some time on our own to think a bit.

It's barely 10 pm and I get into bed, it's been a long day and I can't wait to drift off. Michelle comes in from the bathroom, again, with a big smile on her face. Turning out her lamp she gets into bed and I adjust the duvet to get a little more comfortable. Closing my eyes, I can't wait to see where my dreams are taking me tonight. Suddenly I feel Michelle's hand make its way up my thigh and underneath my boxer shorts. It's been so long and you'd think I'd jump at the opportunity but sadly, I am not in the least bit turned on. Next, she begins kissing my shoulder and still, nothing. I have never had an issue like that before, maybe it's because I am lusting after another woman. Turning toward her, my lips find hers and I wrap my arm around her. With my eyes closed, the image of Shelby biting her lower lip comes to mind and that definitely gets the blood pumping.

Shelby

Hearing Vincent say I was beautiful set something off in me that I can't describe. I am completely falling for this man, a man I cannot have. Why does this have to happen to me? I feel like we have so many things in common, our conversations flow with no awkward moments and when he looks at me, my heart literally skips a beat. We really do enjoy each other's company and that age gap seems to be no obstacle whatsoever. We even listen to some of the same music and enjoy the same kind of movies. One thing that I really love about him is even though he's let loose quite a bit he still has that authoritative thing going on, that comes out once in a while in his tone of voice. I absolutely love that and it's definitely a turn on for me.

Looking at the time on my phone, I'm due for another dose of cold medicine. I figure I better be proactive and try to fight this thing before it's a full-blown cold. Taking the pills and downing an entire glass of water I return to my couch and switch on the TV. While flipping through the channels, I see one of my favorite movies is on and it's just started. These are the times I hate being alone. When I first started dating Chad he was very caring, sweet and attentive. I remember one time when I had the flu and he did everything humanly possible to make me feel better. Where did we go wrong? When was the turning point? Should I have tried harder? Well, it takes two to tango and even if I made mistakes, it wasn't all me. He made the choice to do nothing for months and obviously me breaking off our relationship didn't really matter to him. We didn't even yell at each other. I said my piece and he agreed to leave. Maybe this is what he wanted all along and just didn't want to be the bad guy in that regard.

Sometimes I really wonder if I will ever find happiness with someone. My track record hasn't been the best and now fantasizing about a married man is definitely a path I should be avoiding.

I am awoken by my phone chiming, I guess I must have fallen asleep on the couch. Grabbing it off the coffee table I notice it's already midnight. Focusing my eyes on the sender's name I am surprised that it is from Vincent. Swiping to the side the message pops up, *Goodnight Shelby...I hope you feel better. I just want you to know that I meant every word I said. Sleep well.*

God, why does he have to be so sweet? Obviously, I must have been on his mind as well if he sent me a message, especially at this time of night. What do I respond? Should I respond? After much debating I decide to just send a smiley. Sure, I could have written back half a book of what is going through my head right now but a simple smiley does the job just fine. Thinking about what Kristi said the other night, I may be going at this a little hard. Taking a step back is probably a good idea, or at least the smartest one.

Getting up the next morning I feel a little better but decide to take another dose just to be sure. Getting dressed in my usual skirt and blouse I decide to forgo the perfect makeup look and just apply some mascara and clear lip gloss. A quick braid down the side and that's about all the effort I am going to put into my look today. I'm a secretary, not a model.

Arriving at the office I notice Vincent's car in the parking lot. Am I running late? I usually beat him here. Stepping inside, I smell the coffee as soon as I walk in.

"Good morning Shelby," Vincent says as he walks in my direction. "I got here early and already took care of the coffee. I hope I didn't make it too strong for your liking."

"Wow, thank you. Strong is probably exactly what I need right now," I giggle and he smiles before heading into his office.

As I set my things on the desk, my phone chimes and I wonder who could be messaging me so early in the morning. Digging in my purse I pull it out and see it's a message from Vincent. Wait…I just saw him two seconds ago. Maybe this is from earlier. Now I'm curious and I immediately open it, *Shelby, you look absolutely stunning this morning.* His words warm my heart. Maybe he really likes the more toned-down look I have going on today. I have about twenty different replies I could send back and about half of them are quite witty. I end up just telling him that he just made my day.

Pouring myself a cup of coffee, I sit at my desk and turn on the computer. While I wait for it to boot up, I check to see if any voicemails have been left and it looks as though Mr. Parker's 9 am cancelled. About ten minutes later, Vincent's first client walks in and I ask her to have a seat. Within seconds Vincent appears and calls her back, giving me a quick glance and a smile.

"Hey Shelby, how are you?" John appears, leaning on my desk.

"I'm fine Mr. Baker, and yourself?" I reply.

"Wonderful. Do you have any plans this weekend?" he asks, and I can already tell where this is going.

"I do, pretty tied up actually. Babysitting my niece on Saturday and Sunday my boyfriend and I are visiting his parents. How about yourself?"

"Oh," he pauses. "I thought I overheard a conversation that he was out of the picture."

"We reunited. We realized it wasn't worth throwing everything away after three years."

"Alright, well…that's great to hear. I may go catch a movie or something. Kids are with their mom this weekend."

"Well, they have some cool new releases coming out this week, hope you find something worth watching."

It's great to be quick on your feet, that worked out pretty well. He's invited me out a handful of times in the past but with him just separating from his wife, I will not be the rebound chick. Besides, there is zero attraction there.

At lunch Vincent gathers everyone together at my desk for a quick update to see who is interested in sharing the holiday party with some of the other firms and everyone agrees. This should be pretty fun, I guess it may be time to go dress shopping. The party is set for Saturday, December 17th and that's only a few weeks way. I just wish I had someone to take along with me. Being single at holiday parties always sucks, but who knows, maybe I'll meet some young, hot single lawyer there.

Chapter Seven

Vincent

It's Thursday and Michelle sent me a message saying she and her friends just left for the Hamptons. I hope she has a good time there and can relax just a bit. They've cut a few nurse positions at the clinic so with her being the head nurse she has inherited much more work than she had before. For a moment I think of Monday night, where she actually made a move and we made love. This is the first time I couldn't wait to get it over with and I had a hard time reaching my climax. I'm not exactly sure what it was. In a way I felt as if she just did it because I *'allowed'* her to go on this girl's trip. It didn't feel like she did it because she wanted me.

It's lunchtime and John stops by my office, asking if I'd like to join him at one of our favorite deli's near the office. Figuring it would be good to get out, I agree and grab my blazer off the back of my chair. A moment later, Shelby comes walking into my office with a box of files I asked her to get together. She is beautiful as always, wearing a smile that reaches my heart in an instant. After thanking her, she says she will have the rest of the boxes together by the time I get back from lunch. While eating our sandwiches, John asks why I'm having Shelby pull so many files.

"Well, I'm going to go through some of the older files and archive the ones I can. We're running out of space and I'm sure there are plenty of inactive files that can be stored away."

"Yeah then with our luck, that will be the client that decides they need a lawyer and then we have to dig through them."

"I have a plan. The ones that will be archived will go on a spreadsheet and sorted alphabetically in boxes."

"Oh yeah, that's smart. I remember when we did this with the old boss years ago and it was such a mess."

"Yep, that's why I have a system in mind."

"And when are you going to fit all of this in?"

"Michelle is out of town until Sunday. I'm just going to stay after work," I reply, taking a bite.

"Do you need any help? I may be able to stay today, tomorrow may be a bit tricky,"

"Thank you, John, I think I'll be fine though."

Back at the office, I notice Shelby has definitely been busy. There are ten boxes stacked against the wall behind my desk. Maybe this was a little more than I bargained for, accepting John's help may have been a smart idea after all, I've got a lot of work ahead of me.

It's only 4 pm and we are open for another hour but the afternoon has been so slow that I told everyone they could just go home for the day. I definitely didn't have to say that twice, the office emptied out quite fast. Shelby stops by my office before heading out herself.

"Is there anything else you need before I leave?" she asks. "You're not going home?"

"No, my wife is out of town so I figured I would try to archive all of the old files. I'm going to be here for quite some time," I respond and she steps in to my office.

"I can help you, if you'd like," she offers.

"Thank you, Shelby, I don't want to take up your time. I'm sure you have better things to do," I reply and at that moment she removes her coat and tosses it on one of my armchairs, along with her purse.

"Nonsense, I don't have any plans. I'll stay. Are you hungry? I can order in food if you'd like," she smiles and I have no idea how I am supposed to get any work done with her so close to me.

Shelby orders Chinese food and as we wait for it to be delivered, we get to work. She creates the spreadsheet as I begin pulling files out of the boxes. To be honest, this is actually working out quite well, it will definitely save a lot of time. We've already finished two pages when the delivery driver knocks at the door. After paying, I meet Shelby in the conference room and we dig in. We talk about all sorts of things, vacations, relationships, hopes, dreams. I absolutely love seeing that sparkle in her eye when she talks about things she is passionate about, so full of life.

"So, what is the secret to your marriage?" she asks and I raise my eyebrow. "I mean, twenty-six years is a long time. Do you have a lot in common?"

For a moment I don't know how to respond. Everything inside me is saying just lie to her, tell her Michelle is your soulmate and you know you were destined to be together. I realize I can't do that, I don't want to lie to her. She's not just some acquaintance, I consider her a friend.

"Well Shelby, to tell the truth, it's not easy," I begin. "To be honest, sometimes I feel as if we've turned into roommates and the only thing we do together is eat dinner. It just seems her interest in me has declined and the passion has disappeared entirely."

We lock eyes and it seems as if she either wasn't expecting to hear what she did or she didn't expect me to open up to her in that way.

"Vincent, I am so sorry to hear that," she says before pausing and taking a deep breath. "May I ask you a personal question? If I make you uncomfortable I totally understand if you don't answer."

"Sure," I reply, a little weary on where she is going.

"Is intimacy an issue in your marriage?"

"A big issue," I reply without hesitation, surprising myself a little. "Hence the roommate comment."

"I'm sorry," she begins. "Well, I'm sure my flirtatious way isn't helping you in the least bit."

"You are the only excitement I have in my life right now," I confesses, making her grin a tiny bit.

We continue eating and there's a little bit of a weird silence between us. I completely opened myself up to her, let myself be vulnerable and I'm feeling just a bit exposed right now. A moment later, she lays her chopsticks on the table and sits back in her chair, looking at me.

"I don't get it," she starts, and I cock my head to the side. "You're attractive, attentive, charming and one of the nicest men I've ever met in my entire life. How she isn't interested is beyond me. I would be lucky to find someone like you."

"Wow," I comment and I can't believe she just said that. "Coming from you that means the world to me."

"Why?" she asks.

"Well, you are gorgeous, young, sweet…an old guy like me getting a compliment like that from you is definitely something."

"You're not old," she counters and I chuckle.

"Shelby, I'm fifty," I reply, but she already knew that.

"I don't discriminate," she smiles, making me laugh.

Once we finish eating we return to my office to continue with the files. The next three hours fly by and the conversation has been fun and upbeat. I don't think I've ever laughed this much, it's a nice change. It's getting close to 10 pm so we decide to call it a day. I'm quite surprised that we went through seven of the ten boxes and Shelby offered to stay after work to help out with the rest tomorrow.

Shelby

I am totally exhausted and jump into bed as soon as I get home. Lying there I let the evening run through my head. Hearing how his marriage is slowly going down the drain isn't helping my resolve whatsoever. I told myself to back off a bit but I can't get myself to do it. There is something about him that completely draws me in, wanting to uncover more and more about him. I was completely honest about every word I said, I would be extremely lucky to land someone like him. I've been with so many irresponsible men that I ended up taking care of and would absolutely love to find someone mature and responsible. Maybe I really need to go for an older guy, that may be the secret. God, the way he looks at me makes me weak in the knees. Those eyes…they are so hypnotizing. I was so afraid that I would fall for him, today I realized, I'm beyond falling. I swear, if he would make a move, I wouldn't hesitate for a moment.

The next day at work I have a very hard time concentrating. Every time Vincent walks by, my imagination runs wild and a big part of me would love to experience some of those thoughts running through my mind. I keep telling myself, he is off limits. Then again, it seems as if his wife has lost interest in him and I am definitely more than willing to take on the task of…

"Shelby," I hear a voice rip me out of my thoughts, his voice.

"Oh, Mr. Steele. I'm so sorry I was just spaced out for a moment. Did I forget to do something?" I ask, not able to get an intelligible sentence together.

"No," he laughs. "Just wanted to tell you that your lunch started about fifteen minutes ago. You've been so immersed in your work that I figured you didn't notice."

"Oh, thank you," I say getting up from my desk and grabbing my purse. Yep, I was immersed in something for sure.

As the day comes to an end I toy around with the idea of not staying after work to help with the rest of the files. I could just come up with some stupid excuse like my sister needs a babysitter or something along those lines. Yes…that is exactly what I will do. As I walk toward Vincent's office, John and Bryce pass me, telling me to have a great weekend. Our paralegals already left about a half hour ago leaving just Vincent and me here in the office.

Knocking on the door, Vincent glances at me and his eyes light up, making me smile. I just stand there and stare at him, my mind blank for a moment.

"What is it?" he asks with a smile.

"Um," I begin. "I just wanted to see what you'd like me to order in for dinner."

"Already done," he replies. "The pizza should be here shortly. I hope you like pizza."

"I do," I say with a smile. "Alright, I'll be right back, just have to file a few things away."

God damnit. Good going Shelby, way to stick to your guns. After the pizza arrives we head into the conference room again. Thankfully Vincent is keeping the conversation rolling because for the first time I feel as if I can't really get a sentence together. I love his voice. I could sit here and listen to it all day. The thought of him reading a book to me crosses my mind and it makes me grin a little.

"What's so funny," he asks, a smile on his face.

"Oh nothing," I reply. "You have a great voice. Ever consider doing audio books?"

"Audio books?" he replies, scrunching his forehead.

"Yes, audio books. Seriously, you just have one of those voices that would be perfect for that," I smile and he just shakes his head.

"Wow, I have never heard that before. Thank you. Well, maybe I should look into it," he says winking at me.

After we finish, I get up and pick up our empty paper plates, throwing them into the garbage. Vincent closes the pizza box with the remaining pizza and heads into the breakroom to place it into the refrigerator. We meet in his office and he removes his blazer, hanging it over the chair.

"Alright, are you ready?" he asks as he grabs a stack of folders out of the box on the floor. I nod, sitting down in the chair, bringing up the excel sheet on his computer.

It only takes about an hour and a half to complete the remaining boxes and it's close 8 pm. I shut down the computer as Vincent places the boxes in the corner of the room. I steal a glance and right at that moment our eyes meet. Immediately he looks away, but he reveals a little grin. Again, there is an awkward silence and I'm actually surprised that he breaks it.

"So Shelby, what do you normally do on Friday nights?" he asks.

"Well, once in a while I'll go out with some friends. There's a bar not too far from here where we normally hang out.," I reply, leaning against his desk.

"Oh I'm sorry, I'm sure I kept you from something. You probably had better things to do than go through paperwork with me," he says, looking completely serious.

"Nope, I didn't have anything planned at all, don't worry," I reply. "Besides, I am really happy that I got to spend the last two days with you. I feel like we got to know each other a little better."

"Yes, I agree," he replies.

Another awkward silence. It's almost as if he's waiting for me to make some kind of move. The looks he has been giving me have been a dead giveaway. What do I do? He steps forward placing his phone on the desk, mere inches from me. I feel chills going down my spine and my heart starts to pound. A second later, he turns to look at me. This is my chance, it's now or never. Slowly I place my hand on his cheek and he closes his eyes, inhaling deeply. He leans

72

into the palm of my hand and his lips gently brush my wrist. The feeling of this small intimacy almost takes my breath away. Just a simple touch, yet so beautiful. He opens his eyes and it's as if he is staring into my soul. My heart is racing and my hand travels to the nape of his neck, pulling his lips to mine. The moment we unite is the moment we go from innocence to pure passion. His hands wrap around my waist, pulling me into him. I can feel how much he is longing for this, how much he longs for me. Our tongues are fighting a war and our hands are exploring each other's bodies. I start to undo his tie, tossing it behind me before moving to the buttons on his shirt. Peeling if off his shoulders, I begin kissing his neck, traveling toward his left collarbone. He lets out a loud groan, which tells me he is enjoying the sensation. His breathing picks up and I feel him push me back slightly. He shoots me a little grin and in one swift move he clears one side of his massive desk. Picking me up by my waist he sets me on the edge and begins unbuttoning my blouse, all while his tongue runs down my neck. My hands travel down to his belt, hastily unbuckling it and undoing the button and zipper. Freeing him, I wrap my hand around him, slowly stroking up and down. Moving his mouth away from my neck, he lets out another loud groan and bites his lip. That image is so sexy and the way his eyes are focused on me shoots tingles straight to my groin. I am so ready and I want nothing more than to feel him. I wrap my legs around him, pulling him close. Pushing my skirt up slightly, his hand makes it way underneath, grabbing my panties and ripping the left side off my hip. My hand grips him, guiding him into position and seconds later he fills me, making me cry out. Gripping his shoulders, he kisses me hard as he continues thrusting. Panting and digging my nails into his shoulders, I suddenly feel myself release, screaming his name. That must have set something off in him because his movements become wilder, deeper, more intense and I experience a second orgasm, which takes me by surprise. That has never happened for me before. Hell, reaching one has proven to be difficult at times. The entire time, his lips are on me, trailing kisses. I grip his hair as I feel his teeth graze my neck and moment later he lets out a loud groan and I feel him pulse inside me before his movements slow. Holding each other close, I can feel his heart beating as he runs his fingers through my hair. Then realization hits me. What the hell have we done?

Chapter Eight

Vincent

Sitting in the car, my hands rest on the steering wheel and I am staring out into nothing, still unable to fathom what just happened. Taking a deep breath, I can't help but smile. I still smell her scent on me, so sweet, so intoxicating. To tell the truth, this has been the most thrilling thing I have ever done in my entire life and honestly, I don't regret it. I close my eyes and I can feel her lips on me, kissing me with such longing. I haven't been kissed like that in...I can't even remember.

When she placed her hand on my cheek, I felt so comfortable, as if I've known her my entire life. The way our eyes locked, I swear there is a connection there, that is undeniable. As we pulled away from each other I couldn't help but study her next moves, wondering how she would react. I've never been in a situation like this before so I had no idea what to say. Thankfully she broke the uncomfortable silence, saying that we just got a little carried away. She also said I wouldn't have to worry about anyone ever finding out.

As amazing as it was I just hope it won't complicate our relationship at work. Who am I kidding? How will I ever look at her in any other way again?

When I arrive home the feeling of guilt hits me. Especially after seeing our family picture in the entryway. How will I face my wife after what I've done? Fantasizing about Shelby was one thing, but I have definitely crossed a line. Letting out a deep sigh I place my keys on the key rack and head upstairs to the master bath. A shower is exactly what I need right now. Feeling the hot water stream down my shoulders feels heavenly and for a moment I just let my mind go blank. Suddenly fear creeps into my mind. We didn't use a condom. How could I have been so irresponsible? God, I hope she is on birth control.

Waking up the next morning I feel as if I have been run over by a truck. My thoughts consumed me, never letting me slip into a deep sleep. I get up and go on about my day, well I try to at least. I can't seem to focus on any task I try to accomplish and by the time it's 2 pm I decide to text Shelby, asking if she would be available to talk. I finally get a response about forty-five minutes later with a message reading *Hey sorry I didn't see this until now. Of course, I'm home all day, so you can swing by whenever.* Without hesitation I grab my keys and get into my car. Luke and Ashley are coming by at 6 pm tonight so I need to make sure I'm back before then.

The drive to her apartment takes about thirty minutes but it feels like hours. After finding a place to park, I message Shelby, letting her know I am here and ask what her apartment number is. As I come up to the door I take a deep breath. A part of me is beyond excited to see her again, but the other part would love nothing more than to turn around and not have this awkward conversation. I knock on the door and within five seconds, Shelby stands in front of me, a smile on her face.

"Hey Vincent, come on in," she says, stepping aside.

"Thank you," I reply, as I enter.

Standing in her living room I take a quick glance around. It is very nicely decorated and everything seems to have its place. Even though the building is quite old, this place has a modern flair to it, which I really like.

"Can I get you anything to drink? Coffee, Tea, Water? I think I still have some Orange Juice too," Shelby offers.

"Water would be great," I reply and she walks into the kitchen and takes two glasses out of the cupboard.

I look at a few pictures on a small bookshelf next to the armchair I am sitting in and spot a family photo. I knew she had a sister but it seems she also has a younger brother. Shelby rarely talks about her family and if she does, she doesn't share very much.

"Alright," Shelby says, returning from the kitchen handing me a glass of water. "Sorry I don't have any ice."

"Not a problem," I say, taking a sip before setting it on the table.

"So, you said you wanted to talk?" Shelby asks and I look up at her. God, those eyes of hers are so hypnotizing.

"Yes," I begin. "Yesterday, when I arrived home after…our engagement, I came to realize that I didn't use a condom. I want to let you know that I am disease free. I have never had anything."

"I'm glad to hear that. So am I," she replies with a smile.

"That is wonderful," I pause. "Well, this brings me to my next concern. Shelby, are you on some kind birth control?"

"I am Vincent, no need to worry," she begins. "I know this kind of happened unexpectedly and obviously I know you are married. I want you to know that I will keep this to myself and take it to the grave."

For a moment I don't even know what to say. In a way it seems I really dodged a bullet because this really could tear my entire life apart. How is she so fine about this?

"You're right, we did get carried away," I say, taking a drink of my water.

"To say the least," she says, chuckling before taking a sip of her drink. "Anyway, like I said, I won't tell a soul. We will just continue like before, pretend it never happened."

I give her a smile. That is definitely a relief, but part of me wishes it didn't have to be that way and knowing it will never happen again saddens me a little. It was by far the most amazing experience I've ever had. Well, at least I can say I got to experience it.

Back at home it's close to 6 pm and I'm sure Luke and Ashley will be here shortly. I'm not much of a cook, so a large frozen lasagna it is. Sitting in the recliner catching up on the news, I'm startled when the front door opens and Michelle is home earlier than expected. She had messaged informing me that she and her friends were planning to grab dinner before returning home.

"Hey Vince," I hear her voice coming from the hallway and I get up.

78

"Michelle, I thought you'd be a little later, did you enjoy your trip?'" I ask, trying to sound confident even though I'm a little nervous, knowing I've been with another woman.

"Well, we almost made it to the restaurant when Paula's daughter called needing help with something," she begins. "The trip was wonderful, so relaxing. It was much needed, I feel completely refreshed. What did you do while I was gone?'

"The usual, work. I stayed late archiving files since I never seem to find the time for that during the day."

"Well, that's great. It was beneficial for both of us then. Who's coming for dinner tonight?" she asks, handing me her suitcase to take upstairs.

"Luke and Ashley, I just threw in a frozen lasagna," I reply making my way to the staircase.

"Sounds great, I'll see what else I can throw together."

Shelby

I just pulled into the parking lot at work and a part of me is really nervous about seeing Vincent today. I may have sounded confident and sure of myself during our conversation yesterday but I can't even begin to describe the storm that is brewing inside me. Having him in my apartment, sitting on my couch...it just felt like he belonged there. I really wish things were different.

I get out of my car and notice Vincent pull up. Should I wait and walk in with him? Well, that's what I've done in the past, why change things now. Time to smile and act as if nothing happened...I'm good at that.

"Good morning Mr. Steele," I say as he gets out of his car.

"Good morning Miss Hunter," he replies, throwing me off by using my last name. He never does that. He looks just a bit uncomfortable but before I can say anything else, we are interrupted by John.

"Happy Monday everyone. Everyone have a great weekend?"

"It was alright. I spent most of the weekend cleaning," I respond with a smile.

"Wow," John begins. "Doesn't sound exciting at all. Vince, did you get all of the files squared away?"

"I did," Vincent replies as the three of us make our way up the steps to the office.

Inside, I start my routine by turning on the computer, making coffee and listening to the voicemails left over the weekend. Monday's are usually really busy so I hope it will keep my mind off things. Once the coffee is done I pour everyone their cups and take them to their offices. As I walk into Vincent's office he immediately looks up at me.

"You know, I had a cup at home so I think I will pass today, thank you," he says before his eyes are back to the computer screen.

"No problem," I respond, turning around and walking out of the door.

Wow, that is not what I was expecting this morning. He seems very standoffish and cold. Well, I suppose him calling me Miss Hunter was a good indicator that things have taken a different turn. What was I expecting, he's married. Maybe if he were single things would be just a little different. Oh well, water under the bridge, I can't change how someone feels.

I'm really relieved that the day went by fast and without any more awkward moments. I am still hurt because the fact is, I really like him. On the way home I get a text from my girlfriend Nicole, asking if I'd like to meet her for drinks tonight. I haven't had the chance to hang out with her in a while since she just became a mother four months ago. I did stop by for a visit once her son was born, what a little heartbreaker.

Nicole and I meet at our favorite bar just about five miles from my place. I decided to just take a cab because I definitely feel as if I could use a drink or two. Walking in, I see her waving at me and I make my way to her, giving her a hug before sitting on the stool next to her.

"Oh my god Shelby, it's been months, how are you? You look fantastic," Nicole raves.

"I'm alright. I know we have a lot of catching up to do," I begin, ordering a martini.

"So what's new with you girl? How's Chad?"

"We broke up a few weeks ago," I reply and her eyes widen.

"Wow, I thought you two would end up getting married and have this little picture-perfect family," Nicole says, shocked.

"Nope, wasn't in our future," I reply, taking a drink of my martini. I never really let anyone know about the troubles we had, it's just easier not involving a lot of people.

I'm really glad that we went out tonight, it was so great catching up and hearing about her new adventures of motherhood. Nicole and I used to work together at a nightclub when we were in our late twenties, those were really fun times and it's crazy to see how much our lives have changed over the past few years.

Back at home, I toss and turn all night long, unable to get Vincent off my mind. My sister's words come to mind. She told me to be careful because things could end up in a direction I didn't intend. Truer words were never spoken.

Chapter Nine

Vincent

Today was difficult and I feel terrible for the way I acted towards Shelby. By the look on her face I could tell she was surprised. I think I went a little over the top calling her Miss Hunter, I haven't been that formal with her in months. That one moment of weakness really complicated my entire life, probably hers as well. I'm sitting at the dining table eating a frozen TV dinner since Michelle is at the local coffee shop for her book club. To be honest, it's a relief that she isn't here right now. I have a hard time looking her in the eye, and I hope this guilt will pass.

After finishing my meal, I walk upstairs to my office and figure it's a good time to pay some bills. As I wait for the electric bill to load I glance over to my phone, lying next to the mouse. A part of me wants to send Shelby a message, apologizing for being so cold towards her. Returning my eyes back to the computer screen I enter my credit card information and confirm the payment. I decide against texting Shelby. Tomorrow is a new day, I'll just start over then.

I was asleep before Michelle made it home and I feel so refreshed. I don't remember the last time I last slept eleven hours. Opening the door to the office I see John coming down the hall.

"Morning Vince, better mood today?" he grins.

"What are you talking about?" I reply, my eyes searching for Shelby at the same time.

"Well, you were a bit unapproachable yesterday," John points out.

"Sorry, I just had a few things on my mind," I respond and just then Shelby comes into view.

"Good morning Mr. Steele. Would you like some coffee today?" she asks with a smile.

"Yes please, thank you Shelby," I say.

"My pleasure."

A few minutes later she steps into my office, coffee in hand. Setting it on my desk she asks if there is anything else I need. A million things come to mind, just none that I can voice. Smiling, I tell her that I am all set and a moment later, she is gone. I have to be at court in about an hour so I go over a few last things to refresh my memory. It's nothing major, a traffic violation and to be quite honest, I'm not sure my client is going to show up. He seemed less than enthused during our last meeting. If it weren't for his parents, I don't think he would have even made the effort to search out a lawyer. He just turned eighteen and this is his first speeding ticket. I told his parents that my fees exceed the actual amount of the ticket but they were adamant to have it removed from his record. I doubt that I will win this case but miracles can happen.

It's close to lunchtime and to my surprise, we won. My client was very lucky that he had a lenient judge. I decide to stop to get some lunch on the way back to the office. I brought some chicken salad from home but it doesn't sound like something I want right now. Stepping into the café I notice it is decorated for Halloween. I check the date on my watch and notice that it's this Sunday. The boys usually bring the grandkids to our neighborhood for trick or treating but Libby is invited to a Halloween party at a friend's house and Jackson is with his mom this weekend. That's probably why its slipped my mind, we won't be celebrating this year. Sure, Michelle and I will still hand out candy to children that come to our door but we opted not to decorate.

The rest of the day went by very slow and I've made attempts of having short conversations with Shelby here and there. I found myself missing the way we were, so carefree. Obviously, the incident last Friday complicated things and put a barrier between us which I hope we will be able to overcome.

When I arrive home I expect to find paperwork littering the dining table for Michelle's community meeting, but to my surprise, it's clear. I walk into the kitchen and find her cooking Spaghetti and Meatballs.

"Hey Honey, how was your day today?" I ask, walking over to kiss her, but she turns her cheek to me instead.

"Exhausting, very busy day. I talked to my boss today and said that the workload needs to be distributed a little more evenly otherwise I will be searching out a new job," she replies, placing the lid on the pot.

"You're not preparing for Thursday's meeting?" I ask.

"No, I just don't have the motivation for that tonight. Tomorrow is another day," she replies and I nod.

That's about all of the conversation we have the rest of the night. After dinner Michelle goes upstairs to soak in the tub and I know she will be asleep soon after. She did look very stressed and I hope it will help her relax. As I sit on the sofa I notice it's already 10:30 pm. I haven't really been watching this documentary, my thoughts have been all over the place. Looking over at my phone, I instantly think of Shelby and wonder what she is doing right now.

Shelby

I am so happy that it's Saturday, this past week has been hell. Well, at least half of it. Despite the rocky start on Monday, things between Vincent and I have gone back to normal. At least he can now look me in the eye when he's speaking to me. Obviously, the flirting has stopped all together, which is for the best anyway. I think we got a little too friendly with each other, too familiar, too careless. Even though things are toned down it doesn't mean that I don't lust after him every single day. His wife sure is a lucky woman, but apparently doesn't realize it. I would do anything to be in her shoes.

Right now, I am sitting at my dining table scrolling through my phone, re-reading old messages Vincent sent me. God, I want him so bad. I take a deep breath and decide to go for a run at a nearby park to clear my head a little. I don't run very often but it does help when my thoughts are all over the place. Walking into my bedroom I change into my leggings and black hoodie, putting my hair up into a ponytail. Luckily the park is only two blocks away so I don't need to use my car. Today is a bit chilly so I am surprised to see so many people out walking. After about two miles and some really great music I decide it's time to cool down a bit. I have about a quarter mile before I get back to my starting point. For a moment my eyes make their way to a bench with a man sitting there deep in thought. Taking a closer look, I realize that it's Vincent.

What is he doing here? Why does he look so troubled? Should I say hi?

After debating for about ten seconds, I decide to see if everything is okay. Removing my earbuds from my ears I walk over to him.

"Vincent?" I say and he immediately looks up at me.

"Shelby?"

"Is everything alright?" I ask concerned, sitting down next to him.

"Not really," he exhales. "My wife and I got into a huge argument. I just had to get away for a bit. Be on my own."

"Oh I'm sorry, I shouldn't have both-" I apologize, but before I can get up, I feel his hand on my wrist.

"No please, you're not bothering me," he replies with a smile.

"Your hands are freezing; how long have you been sitting here?"

"About thirty minutes," he responds.

"How would you feel about having some coffee? If you want to talk about it, I'll listen," I offer and he grins.

"Sure," he replies.

"Alright, so I can either make us a cup at my place or we can go to the little coffee shop about three blocks down the road. I'll just have to go home and change though," I explain.

"Whichever is easier for you, I'm fine with your coffee," he says and I get up from the bench.

To my surprise he is actually quite chatty on the way to my apartment, mainly talking about work. We arrive within ten minutes and I unlock my door and we walk inside. I tell him to make himself comfortable as I go into the kitchen to start the coffee maker. When I come back into the living room I see him standing in the middle of the room and our eyes meet. I feel as if I'm frozen in place, unsure what to say, what to do. What happens next completely catches me off guard. He walks over to me and runs his hand down the side of my face while the other lightly grips my waist. One touch from him and I react, wrapping my arms around his neck, pulling him in for a kiss. The moment our lips meet, electricity jolts through my body and I don't ever want to let him go again. His hand moves up under my sweatshirt, running up my ribcage. He breaks our kiss for a moment asking where my bedroom is and I grab his hand, leading him there. Grabbing my shoulders, he kisses me again before gently pushing me back so I am sitting on the bed. He then removes my sweatshirt, along with my sports bra and lets out a small groan. Pulling his shirt over his head he moves on to his pants, unbuckling the belt and undoing the button along with the zipper. Next, he gently pushes me back and his hands move to my hips. His fingers slip under the waistband of my leggings, sliding them and my panties off at the same time. Climbing on top of me, he moves me further back on to the bed so we are more comfortable. He begins kissing me, starting at my neck, leading further down until he reaches my hips. My hand is in his hair and my breathing has picked up in excitement. A part of me is wondering if I am dreaming right now, but when he returns his lips to my mouth I realize this isn't a dream at all. Within moments we are lost in each other, making love. There is nothing rushed about this and the connection I feel to him is one of the strongest I've ever experienced in my entire life. As he moves he whispers that I am the most beautiful thing he's ever seen, completely melting me. This is very different from the first time and even though that encounter was breathtaking, this is intoxicating and I never want it to end. The way he caresses my entire body, the way he touches me, the look in his eyes. He's already sent me over the edge several times and I can tell he is close to reaching his peak. He begins to pant, driving me wild and within seconds his lips search mine for a deep kiss before he explodes. Lying next to each other, I feel his arm around me, pulling me in. He kisses my forehead and my hand is on his chest, slowly moving up and down.

"Wow," he comments, still breathing hard.

"I agree," I reply, recovering myself.

A part of me is a little worried about what is about to happen next. I assume he's going to get up, regret what just happened and run out of here. To my surprise, he just lays here with me in his arms, holding me close. My hand reaches for the blanket on the bottom of my bed, covering us both. About ten minutes later, he breaks the silence.

"Shelby?"

"Yes?" I reply, alright, here we go.

"I've come to the realization that I have a hard time controlling myself around you. I've never done anything like this before but there is this magnetic pull, bringing me towards you, I don't know how to explain it," he says and I'm relieved.

"I know what you mean. I feel the same way. This last week has been so difficult. You were on my mind the entire time."

"God…what are we going to do?"

"I don't know Vincent," I begin. "I really love being with you and I know this is wrong, but I don't want to lose you, even if I'm being unrealistic."

"You're not being unrealistic, I feel the same way. I don't want to give you up Shelby," he says, kissing my head and I snuggle closer to him.

Chapter Ten

Vincent

This time I don't feel guilty as I get into my car. How did she become so important to me so quickly? Before leaving I send her a quick message, telling her that she is in my heart and I'll be thinking of her.

As I drive away, I can't get the image of Shelby lying in my arms out of my head. I swear it must have been fate that we bumped into each other at the park. The last time I was there was maybe eight years ago and I'm not entirely sure what pulled me to that specific one. I could have never pictured myself having an affair but it seems that is the journey I am embarking on.

I figured that the guilt would hit me as soon as I saw Michelle, but it didn't. I asked if she wanted to talk about our fight earlier and she just gave me the cold shoulder and walked out of the room. Our fight was about remodeling the kitchen. We just had it updated less than two years ago. At the time Michelle really wanted a modern look but apparently now she prefers the rustic flair. This is purely cosmetic and has nothing to do with functionality and I just don't see spending tens of thousands of dollars for looks. Over the years I've never denied her much but there have been cases I have put my foot down, especially if the idea is ridiculous.

About ten minutes later there is a knock at the door and I go to see who it is. To my surprise I see Ashley and Libby standing there and I tell them to come inside.

"We thought we'd just stop by because we were in the area shopping, are you guys busy?" Ashely asks.

"Oh no, not at all," Michelle says as she walks over to us. "Ashely do you want some coffee?"

"No thank you, I grabbed a cup while I was out," Ashley smiles and they walk into the living room.

Ashley and Michelle have always gotten along very well and she's almost become the daughter we never had. I decide to let them have their time together and retreat to my office upstairs. Removing my phone from my pocket I lay it on my desk and I see that I have a message waiting for me. Swiping the screen, I see the the that the message is from Shelby. *You have a special spot in my heart as well and I know you will be on my mind until I see you again.*

Reading that sends a feeling of joy through me, and I can't help but smile. I feel so close to her and find myself missing her already. A thought crosses my mind, it may be a good idea to set a passcode on my phone, just in case. My intention was to work on a few projects when I came up here but Shelby and I have been messaging each other for the past hour, time really does fly. About five minutes later Michelle is standing in the doorway, telling me dinner is ready.

Just as I assumed, there wasn't going to be much conversation going on during our meal. I can tell she is still in a bad mood and part of me just wants to give in and let her do whatever she wants, in a way it would make my life easier. Debating for a moment I come to the conclusion that I am going to stick to my guns, I'm not a pushover.

The rest of the weekend went by in a blur. Michelle finally gave up the attitude but I know the issue will come up again. We didn't have as many trick or treaters this year. It was really cold outside, maybe that's the reason why. I am on my way to work and I can't wait to see Shelby. Her and I have been in contact all weekend and every time one of her messages pops up, I start to grin. I haven't felt wanted in years, I had no idea how much I actually missed it.

Pulling into the parking lot, I notice Shelby is already there and quickly make my way inside the office. Setting my briefcase on the desk and removing my blazer I hear that slight knock on the door and I know exactly who it is.

"Mr. Steele," she says and I look up. She's wearing her hair down today and looks even more beautiful to me than before.

"Good morning Shelby," I respond with a smile and she comes in, coffee in hand, closing the door quietly.

Setting my coffee on the desk, she wraps her arms around my neck and within seconds we are lost in a kiss. This is definitely something I can get used to but we do need to make sure we control ourselves. A moment later she backs away just a little, her hand on my tie, tugging gently.

"I see you're wearing your lucky tie," she winks. "My favorite."

"I remember you mentioning that you liked it, that's why I chose to wear it," I reply and she kisses my cheek before leaving the office. God, how am I going to focus on anything today?

"Hey Vince," John says as he steps into my office. "You look happy, did you have a good weekend?"

"You could say that," I reply, my thoughts taking me back to Shelby's apartment.

"Yeah mine was alright, I went out on another date," he starts. "With Donna."

"Donna as in your wife?" I ask, surprised.

"Yep, we may give our marriage another shot. It's definitely cheaper to keep her."

"Well, I hope it works out. How long have you two been married again?" I ask, not really knowing what else to say.

"Nineteen years. Nothing compared to you and Michelle. She must be a saint for putting up with you," he laughs and I chuckle.

It's close to 3 pm and Shelby steps into my office with tomorrow's files. Placing them on my desk she looks me in the eye, biting her lower lip.

"Phew," I sigh.

"Yes, Mr. Steele?" she replies, flirtatiously.

"God, I want you right now," I say, surprising myself.

"Well, I feel the same way," she begins. "I do believe it would be safer in say, a more private place. My apartment for example."

"I agree 100%," I reply.

"So, obviously it's a little more difficult on your end for obvious reasons," she says with a bit of a frown.

"You're right," I say, trying to come up with a plan and a moment later it hits me. "Do you have any plans after work today?"

"I don't," she says with a mischievous look in her eye. "Are you paying me a visit?"

"If you'll have me," I respond and she smiles.

"Hmm…let me think about that one," she grins before leaving my office.

God there was something so sexy about the way her eyes focused in on me while saying that, I'm not sure I've ever felt this alive. Today would be perfect, Michelle is meeting with her book club at the coffeeshop after work so she won't know if I'm there or not. In case she makes it back before I do, I can just say that I had to work late. I throw myself into my work and before I know it, it's 5 pm and I haven't seen any sign of Shelby. Maybe she didn't want me to come by and just wasn't sure how to tell me. I can't imagine that I was too forward. Shutting down my computer, I grab my blazer from the back of my chair.

"Mr. Steele?" I hear Shelby's voice as she steps into my office.

"Yes?" I reply, smiling at her.

"Well, I'm heading out. I just wanted to see if there is anything else you needed."

"Actually yes," I respond, slowly walking over to her. She cocks her head to the side, curiosity written all over her face. "Just wondering if you've had enough time to think."

"Oh," she says, eyes widened. "I just assumed that you would take it as a yes. Sorry, sometimes I like to toy around like that."

"It was hot," I reply and she winks at me.

"Alright, I plan to see you shortly then. Make sure you bring that tie."

Shelby

Vincent should be here any minute and I definitely have something in mind for him today. Through our conversations I found out that he hasn't had the opportunity to experiment very much sexually. It seems as if it's more of a chore than a pleasure for his wife, and I for the life of me can't understand why. Both times I've been with him were breathtaking to say the least. I suppose to each their own.

I go into the bathroom to freshen up just a bit but I stay in my work attire, heels and all. A moment later, the doorbell rings and I go to answer it.

"Hi Vincent," I say, wrapping my arms around him, kissing him deeply.

Once inside, I take his hand and lead him into my bedroom. Immediately he tries to take control but that won't be happening today. I turn him around so the back of his knees are against the bed, and with my hands on his shoulders, slowly push him down so he is sitting on the edge. Grabbing his hands, I move them to the back of my skirt, asking him to help me with the zipper. As my skirt falls to the ground his hands move to the buttons of my blouse, slowly undoing each one. Pulling me closer, he kisses my hips before moving up my abdomen, his hands running up my ribcage to my breasts. I inhale deeply, my head falling back, enjoying every kiss, every touch. I feel him unclasping the garter belt from my stockings and that is when I playfully slap his hand. He looks at me, full of surprise and I lean close to his ear, whispering for him to be patient. He takes a deep breath and leans back on his hands, palms on the bed. I proceed to remove my blouse and panties, leaving the garter and stockings on. Next, I start on him, undoing his tie, wrapping it around my wrist for later use. Once I have him out of his clothes, I can see he's ready, who am I kidding? I knew he was there the moment he walked in the door. I ask him to get on the bed and lie down, straddling him I lean forward to kiss his lips. I feel his hands on my lower back, grasping, longing for me. Next, I unwrap the tie from around my wrist and he looks at me a little perplexed.

"Are you planning on tying me up?" he asks, a bit of fear in his voice.

"No," I reply. "Do you trust me?"

He stares into my eyes and is silent, debating. Maybe we aren't quite there yet, I think to myself. Before I can say anything, he speaks.

"I trust you Shelby."

I smile, leaning down to kiss him before using the tie to blindfold him. I really think he is going to enjoy this, actually, I am quite confident. Once I'm certain he can't see a thing I begin running my tongue down his neck, gently nibbling his collarbone. My hand runs down from his other shoulder, over his heart which is now beating uncontrollably. I continue spoiling him with my lips and I feel his body react, finding all of his sensitive areas. Just when he least expects it I envelop him entirely, moving back and forth, taking his hands and placing them on my hips. He starts to groan; his grip tightens and he begins guiding me back and forth. We find a perfect rhythm and it doesn't take long before I feel myself explode, moaning loudly. His hands continue to move my hips and I feel him pulsate, knowing he is close.

"Come here," I hear him sigh, grabbing my arms and pulling me close to him. Our lips connect and within second our kiss deepens, tongues entangled. With his arms still wrapped around me, I continue moving until moments later he reaches his peak, groaning against my neck. We stay in that position, catching our breath. Collapsing next to him, he removes the blindfold and pulls me close to him.

"That was incredible," he says, kissing my shoulder. "You are incredible."

"I can only give you the same compliment," I say, laying my head on his chest, my fingertips on his hip. "Vincent?"

"Yes, love," he responds, making me smile at the term of endearment.

"Say something to me in Ukrainian," I say and he chuckles.

"Okay," he inhales. "Ty taka vrodlyva."

"That sounds beautiful. What does it mean?" I ask.

"You are so beautiful."

Chapter Eleven

Shelby

Vincent always tells me I'm beautiful, but hearing him say it in a different language just melts me. I don't consider myself beautiful, just average. I've seen tons of gorgeous women around the city and I know I can't compete with them. I'm comfortable enough in my own skin but still feel myself blush when he pays me those compliments.

God, I already miss him. I wish he could just stay here with me but I know that's impossible. Who knows, maybe his wife will decide to go on another trip sometime. I would give anything just to be able to wake up next to him once. Well, I better get used to this really quick, he's not my boyfriend, he can't be. Sure, he's my lover but I can't just stop by his house or call him when I miss him. Thank God for texting.

It's Thursday and work has been non-stop. Usually we will have a few cancellations here and there but everyone decided to keep their appointment this week. Even though I haven't had much of a chance to talk to Vincent during the workday, he makes sure to send me messages during most of the evening. Sometimes we end up talking until midnight. I really feel like I am starting to fall in love with him, I guess it's inevitable.

My sister Kristi invited me over for dinner tonight and I'm happy I'll get to see Hayley again. The older she gets the busier she is. I get it though, even though I am her favorite aunt, I can't keep up with her friends, nor would I want to. I stop by Vincent's office before leaving, telling him goodbye and sneaking in a kiss. It's not something I can do every day, there are times where it would just be too risky and I settle for that gorgeous smile of his.

Pulling up to my sister's house, I see an unfamiliar car in the driveway and wonder who it could be. She didn't tell me they were having other guests over. I get out of my car and walk to the door, ringing the bell. Kristi's husband Adam answers and tells me to come inside.

"Who else is here?" I ask as I hang my coat in the closet and remove my shoes.

"Just my coworker, his wife and kid. You'll love them," Adam says, grabbing the dessert I brought.

"Oh, that's right, you just started your new job last month," I say as we walk into the living room.

A moment later I freeze as I recognize Adam's coworker. I've never met him but recognize him from a picture, hell, even if I never saw the picture, he is a young Vincent.

"So, this is Kristi's sister Shelby. Shelby this is Luke, Ashley and their daughter Libby," Adam announces, as Kristi walks in with a casserole.

"Hey Shelby, perfect timing. Alright everyone, let's go sit down and eat. Adam, can you grab the rolls off the counter?"

As we all sit down at the table, I start to feel very uncomfortable. How am I going to get through this dinner? Essentially, Luke is a stranger to me and I should treat him as such but my relationship with his father is definitely making this whole situation a little weird. Well, let's just hope my job doesn't come up.

We are halfway through dinner and I direct most of my conversation at Hayley and Libby while my sister chitchats with Ashely. Adam and Luke are talking about work related stuff and if things continue this way, I definitely dodged a bullet. About five minutes later that dream ends.

"Hey Shelby, what do you do workwise?" Ashley asks while Kristi goes into the kitchen to grab the pie that I brought.

"Umm...I'm a secretary," I reply and now Luke gets in on the conversation.

"Where do you work?" he asks while trying to get his daughter to take a bite of her food.

"A law office downtown," I say and right now I just want to get out of here.

"Luke's dad is a lawyer. What office do you work for?" Ashley asks as Kristi returns with the pie.

"Steele and Baker," I say, wiping my mouth with the napkin, thinking it may be inaudible. Kind of stupid since I'm sure they would just ask again.

"Oh my God! Small world. My dad owns that firm. Vincent Steele. That's crazy, you work for my dad," Luke says with a big smile and suddenly he and his wife look at me like we have this great connection.

"Wow, yeah small world. So, Ashely, what do you do?" I say, trying to take the attention off me.

"I just work part-time at a daycare. Libby goes there on the days I work so it's very convenient," Ashley smiles.

"Shelby, do you want any dessert?" Kristi asks, looking at me.

"No thank you, I have to get going anyway so-"

"Oh, come on, we were going to play a card game in a bit, you can't go," Adam pleads.

"Well, we're an odd number of people anyway so it wouldn't work," I say and then I'm informed that the number of players doesn't matter in this game. Great.

Kristi hands me a piece of pie and the conversation continues. My phone chimes, letting me know I have a message and I know it has to be from Vincent. Thankfully I placed it under my thigh on the chair. As Adam and Kristi start to clear the table, I check the message and it was Vincent, asking if I'm enjoying dinner. I send him a quick message back, telling him I will tell him about it in the morning.

After Hayley and Libby go to play in Hayley's playroom, Kristi gets the card game out and explains the rules. Seems pretty straight forward, we each get ten cards containing anything from words to small sentences. One player sits out each round and plays a separate card that includes a sentence with a blank. The other players fill in the blank by placing the funniest card on the table, facedown, while the *'sitting out'* player looks away. Once all cards are on the table they are flipped and the non-player chooses the best card.

As I look through my cards of course I would end up with the terms AFFAIR, FRIENDS WITH BENEFITS and FATHER. At least my others are random, like FINGER PAITING and THREE DICKS AT THE SAME TIME. I can already tell this is going to be an interesting game.

Vincent

Unfortunately, I wasn't able to talk to Shelby much last night since she was at her sister's. Her texts seemed just a bit short so I hope everything was alright. I woke up unusually early this morning and figured I would head to the office. Things between Michelle and I are back to normal with everyone doing their own thing. At least she stopped talking about the kitchen renovation. The issue came up one more time mid-week and we were able to have a normal conversation about it this time around. I think she finally understands that it is a waste of money.

I stopped by the bakery this morning and picked up a dozen donuts as a treat for the staff. Shelby usually brings things in but she mentioned that she wouldn't have the time to bake anything after getting back from her family.

"Oh donuts, yum," Bryce comments, walking into the breakroom and grabbing one.

Walking towards the coffee maker, I decide to get that started as well. Just as I measure out the coffee Shelby walks in.

"Good morning Mr. Steele, looks like you're doing my job again," she smiles.

"I got here really early so why not help out. I brought donuts too, they are in the breakroom," I start. "So how was dinner?"

"I need to tell you that privately," she whispers and I'm guessing it must be some family issue she doesn't want everyone to know.

At 10 am I finally have a break and since everyone else is tied up, this is the perfect time for her to tell me what happened. I step out of my office and walk toward her desk and sit down on the chair next to her desk.

"So, what happened?" I ask curiously.

"Well, you'll never believe this. My brother-in-law invited a coworker and his family over and it happened to be your son," she says and it takes me a moment to register what she just said.

"Luke?" I reply and she nods her head. "Wow, I'm sure that was...quite awkward."

"Oh yeah, I was hoping my job wouldn't come up but then Ashely asked what I do for a living and it went downhill from there," she explains.

"So, he knows that you work for me," I say and she nods again. "Don't worry about it. You didn't tell anyone about us, right?"

"No, I didn't," I start. "Months ago I told my sister that I flirted around with you here and there but that's it. Nothing since," she replies.

"See, everything will be alright then. I'm just sorry that I put you in that positi-" I apologize and before I can say thing else, she interrupts me.

"Don't apologize, neither of us could have known. Yeah it was a little weird but I survived," she smiles.

To be honest, it came as a shock to me as well. We live in a big city, what are the chances that my son would be working with her brother-in-law.

A few weeks go by and we are coming up on Thanksgiving. Shelby and I are still seeing each other and I couldn't be happier. I've grown so close to her that I couldn't imagine life without her anymore. It definitely isn't easy to find some alone time together. We usually meet at her apartment Monday's after work and sometimes I can swing a Saturday here and there. When that doesn't work we've utilized our lunch hour on more than one occasion. Those times are definitely steamy but since we are rushed for time, it doesn't compare to the moments we get to lie in each other's arms after.

Today is Saturday and it happens to be a busy one for us here at home. My in-laws just flew in from Minnesota and are visiting for the week to celebrate Thanksgiving with us. It will be nice having both sides of the family together but a major drawback is that Michelle asked if I could take the week off along with her. Of course, I obliged but I already know I am going to go stir crazy, especially not being able to see Shelby for so long. Sitting at my desk I stare out the window.

Again, I find myself thinking of her, longing to be in her presence. Seeing her smile is the highlight of my day. Knowing I placed that smile on her lips gives me a feeling of pure bliss. Yet, she isn't mine and I cannot be hers. Well, technically speaking. She has 100% of my heart and I know that I reside in hers.

Chapter Twelve

Shelby

Today is Thanksgiving and I haven't seen Vincent in six days. Not having him at work is so hard. We've been messaging one another a lot and he snuck in a phone call one night as well which really surprised me. It was so good to hear his voice, I could just close my eyes and drift away, it is so calming. Before hanging up, he whispered something to me in Ukrainian again but wouldn't reveal what it was, saying I'd just have to wait until Monday.

I just got to my sister's house with the Stuffing and Pecan pie. I can't wait to see my brother, it's been so long. About ten minutes later, the bell rings and I go to answer since everyone else has their hands full.

"Hi Sweetie," my mom shrieks, pulling me in for a hug and my dad grabs me next. They only live about an hour away but we don't see each other very often.

"Shelby!" I hear my brother and a second later he picks me up off the ground, giving me a tight squeeze.

"Wow, Matt have you been working out? Your arms are massive," I comment as he sets me back on the ground.

"Oh, you know, a little here and there," he smiles and they come inside.

Once Kristi, Adam and Hayley join us we go into the living room to sit down and catch up. Matt tells us he's met someone and he's thinking about getting engaged. Her name is Katherine and they met a little over nine months ago. She was supposed to join him on this trip as a surprise but had a family emergency and couldn't make it.

"Shelby, I know it's been a few months but are you seeing anyone since breaking up with Chad?" my mom asks and I shake my head.

"No, I'm taking a break from dating. Just focusing on myself and my job for now," I reply.

Dinner was amazing and I feel like I am unable to move. I should have passed on the pie, I'm sure that was the tipping point. My parents and brother are spending the night here tonight and I think I really don't feel like driving home either. Hayley has a bunk bed and she loves it when I sleep over.

Right now, we are all sitting on the couch watching a movie. Taking out my phone I discreetly take a picture of the TV in front of me and send it to Vincent. About ten seconds later I get a reply, saying they are watching the same thing at the moment. What a coincidence.

We spend the rest of the evening having a few drinks, catching up and having a lot of laughs. Once everyone decided to go to bed, Matt asks if I would like to join him out on the patio. Matt is a smoker and our sister would kill him if he did that in the house. Grabbing our hats and coats we step outside and sit on the wicker chairs.

"It's actually less cold than it was earlier," Matt comments, as he lights a cigarette.

"Yeah, I think you're right," I reply, removing my hat.

"So now that it's just us, who are you seeing?" Matt asks, looking me straight in the eye.

"No one Matt, what are you talking about?"

"Bullshit Shelby. Your phone has been buzzing all night and every time you check it, you have this big smile on your face. Mom and Dad may be delusional, well Kristi too, but I'm on to you sis."

A second later my eyes are on the ground and a grin comes over my lips. Even though he is so much younger, he's always been able to see right through me.

"Yep, I knew it. Your silence says it all. Don't worry, I won't pry. Obviously, you want to keep it to yourself. I'm guessing this guy makes you happy?" Matt asks.

"Extremely," I sigh.

"Alright, that is what's important," Matt smiles. "So why did things end with Chad? It didn't have anything to do with what happened to you years ago, does it?'

"God no. Nothing like that. He walked out on his job and decided to start drinking. After I noticed that things weren't going to change I ended it. I just told everyone that our relationship just ran its course and we split mutually. In a sense, we did, he didn't mind leaving."

"So, have you mentioned what happened to you to this new guy?" Matt asks and I shake my head.

Nodding, Matt changed the subject and talks about his new girlfriend for a bit. There is a good reason why I kept the real reason of our breakup from my parents. My dad has been an alcoholic for years, the main reason he kept losing his job, making us move from place to place. He never was a mean drunk and I would almost say he was a functioning alcoholic. My mom always did her best to sugarcoat everything, my dad could do no wrong in her eyes. If I told her I threw three years away for that reason, she wouldn't have understood. She really liked Chad.

Once Matt finishes his cigarette we walk back into the house, locking the patio door. Quietly I open the door to Hayley's room and get into the bottom bunk. It's a little late but I still text Vincent goodnight. It's become a little ritual of ours. A few seconds later I get a message back and it reads **Goodnight darling. I miss you and can't wait to see you.**

Vincent

It has been great having the entire family here for Thanksgiving. We haven't had the house this full in years. Michelle's parents have never met Jackson and within minutes he had them wrapped around his finger. Michelle and her mom took care of all of the cooking and they outdid themselves. We had so much food that we could have fed another family. Mom brought her famous *Medovik*, better known as a Honey Cake. She only makes it once or twice a year since it's a bit of a process, but it's one of the best desserts I've ever had.

Even though I've enjoyed having everyone here I find my thoughts drifting to Shelby, wondering how she is doing. I really miss seeing her beautiful smile, feeling her touch. I scold myself for having these thoughts, especially when my entire family is around. This is so wrong, I know it is. I'm sure you're thinking, well, if you think it's so wrong then end this madness, pick one. It's not that easy. I've never imagined that I would be involved in a situation like this and now I can say I completely understand others that have. On one side I have my wife. She's beautiful, kind, a great mother and we've been together so many years that it would be hard to imagine my life without her. Then there's Shelby. Aside from being beautiful, she warms my heart, makes me laugh and I feel as if I come alive with her. The lack of connection I feel with Michelle has been replaced by Shelby and to be honest, I am much happier than I was months ago. Yet, I do know I can't keep this up forever, nor would I want to. Even though I am very happy, this also causes a lot of stress on me.

It's Friday morning and all of the women in the house decide to fight the crowds on Black Friday. I went one year and I saw enough for a lifetime, and besides, I'm not much of a shopper. I grab my phone off the nightstand and see I have a message notification. Immediately I smile, knowing it must be from Shelby. Unlocking my phone, I click the message app and I was right. A good morning message along with a picture. This must be her brother that she told me about the other week.

Replying back, I ask why they aren't out shopping along with the rest of the city and within seconds I get a reply saying *My brother, niece and I are holding down the fort while the rest of the family deals with the craziness.*

We message back and forth for a bit before I get up and jump in the shower. About ten minutes later I walk downstairs and as I pass the guest room, my father-in-law opens the door.

"Morning Vince, no shopping for you?" he asks jokingly.

"Oh no," I reply, "I'm not much of a shopper in general anyway. Are you hungry? I can make some eggs if you'd like."

"That sounds great, thank you Vince. I'll be down in a minute."

As I get the carton of eggs out of the refrigerator, I hear the front door open. Michelle and her mom walk into the kitchen, bags in tow.

"Well, it looks as if you were successful," I comment and Michelle sets her bags on the floor.

"I was actually disappointed. Not very many deals out there," Michelle replies.

"We did get a few good things though," Michelle's mom smiles.

Michelle's dad joins us and after I finish making breakfast for the four of us, we all sit at the dining table. Michelle's mom said she couldn't believe how crowded the stores were, they are from a very small town in Minnesota so it isn't even comparable. As the conversation continues, I am lost in thought, reflecting on this past week. Even though we've been having a wonderful time with the family, it seems that every time Michelle and I are alone, she tries her hardest to pick a fight. It seems as if every little thing I do, or don't do, sets her off. Maybe this has nothing to do with a new kitchen, she may just be unhappy in this relationship as well.

"Vince, how about we take mom and dad to the Seafood Market for dinner tonight?" Michelle suggests.

"Sounds like a great idea. What time would everyone like to go? I think it would be a good idea to make reservations," I reply and we decide on 6 pm.

Chapter Thirteen

Shelby

It's been ten days since I've seen Vincent and even though we've been messaging each other the entire time, I've missed him terribly. I can't wait to wrap my arms around him and just hold him, even just a moment.

As I pull up to the office, I notice I am the first one here. Getting out of the car I make my way up the steps and unlock the door. Vincent gave me a key after leaving my wallet at my desk that one time. I remember feeling terrible for asking him to come in on a Saturday. Turning on all the lights, I walk toward the coffee maker and start my morning ritual. Five minutes later, I hear the front door open and my heart starts to pound in anticipation. Great, it's John.

"Morning Shelby, how was your Thanksgiving?" John asks.

"It was great, and yours Mr. Baker?"

"It was wonderful. The wife and I decided to work things out so it was just us and the kids," he replies.

"That's great to hear, I am happy for you. Would you like some coffee? It should be done momentarily," I offer and he nods.

As I add the sweetener to John's coffee, I see Bryce walk in and after saying good morning I'm surprised that he asks for coffee as well. Since working here, I've never seen him have any. Once I deliver both cups I hear the phone ring and rush back over to my desk. While on the phone, the front door opens again and immediately I smile. Vincent is wearing that blue striped tie that I love but seeing the spark in his eyes immediately makes me weak. As he comes up to my desk, he stops and waits for me to finish up on the phone.

"Alright Mrs. Johnson, I have you down for an appointment with Mr. Preston on Wednesday at 10 am. Is there anything else I can help you with?" I ask, dying to get off this phone. "Alright, I hope you have a wonderful day and we will see you on Wednesday. Goodbye."

"Good morning Shelby," Vincent says with a grin on his face.

"Good morning Mr. Steele," I reply. "Would you like some coffee this morning?"

"Yes please," he replies, walking toward his office, but stopping before entering. "Oh Shelby, I have a matter I need to discuss with you, it won't take long."

"Yes sir," I reply, wondering what he's talking about. "I will be there in just a moment."

As I pour the coffee, a part of me wonders if I screwed something up. His tone was a little strong. Well, I guess I'm about to find out.

As I stand in the doorway, coffee in hand he looks up and smiles.

"Could you please close the door behind you?" he asks and I shut the door.

Walking towards his desk, I set the cup on it and he gets up, coming around the desk to meet me. A second later one of his hands is on my hips and the other on the back of my head pulling me in for a kiss. Immediately I start to melt, kissing him back, my hands on his back, pulling him even closer to me. After what feels like forever, Vincent pulls back and looks at me.

"I missed you, darling."

"I missed you too," I say. "I have to say, I thought I did something wrong when you said you needed to speak to me."

"Oh no. I just wanted to take the opportunity to hold you at least once today."

"Oh, you won't be coming over after work?" I ask and he sighs.

"Unfortunately, I won't be able to," he replies, looking disappointed.

"Oh ok," I reply, disappointed myself. "Well, I'm glad we had this moment then. Oh, I almost forgot, you said you'd reveal the translation of what you told me on the phone the other day."

"Oh, that's right. Ty napovnyuyesh moye zhuttya."

"It sounds so beautiful," I sigh.

"It means, you fulfill my life," he smiles and I immediately pull him close to me, giving him one more long kiss before heading back to my desk.

Sitting at my desk, I start working and finally catch a break about two hours later. I was really looking forward to spending some time with Vincent this afternoon but I guess that's off the table now. These are the times I really dislike being the other woman. I obviously can never come first since no one is supposed to know about me. I wonder if it's possible that he and his wife may have reconnected during their time off, it's definitely possible.

When I get home, I decide to go for a run in the park. It's been a long day and even though it is freezing out, I feel as if I could really use some fresh air and clear my head. After completing two miles my lungs have taken all they can and now I'm feeling a stinging pain, damn cold weather.

As soon as I get back, I rush into the shower and the hot water running down my body feels like heaven. I've had so many thoughts run through my head and my run really didn't make it any better. Well, at least I can allow myself to have a piece of the cheesecake I have sitting in my refrigerator.

I have the hardest time falling asleep. Lying on my bed, one thought consumes my mind...how did we get here? Had anyone told me this was the path my life would take I would have scrunched my forehead and deemed them insane. Yet, my feelings for him grow stronger each day and this journey only makes me want to discover more.

Taking a deep breath, I realize that he's become something I never expected…the center of my entire world.

Vincent

I toss and turn, unable to find sleep. All I see are Shelby's eyes, full of disappointment staring back at me. Even though she concealed her sadness with a smile, I know she was looking forward to me coming over. She and I haven't had any time to ourselves in almost two weeks and I wanted nothing more than to spend at least a few hours with her lying in my arms. My schedule is incredibly busy this week as well, so I doubt we will be able to take an extended lunch. I'll have to figure something out, there is no way I can wait until the weekend. To be honest, I'm not even sure I will be able to see her on Saturday. Michelle needs a new dress for our office Christmas party and I promised we would spend the day in Manhattan. Luke mentioned that he and Ashley may want to join us as well since they have a party to attend the weekend before ours.

Just as I predicted. The week has been insanely busy and it's been tough to even have a private conversation with Shelby. We end up messaging each other during most of the day, even though we are only about twenty feet from one another. I've spent my entire day at court today and I'm on my way back to the office. I'm sure everyone is getting ready to leave since it's already 5 pm but I'm hoping to at least tell Shelby goodbye. As I pull up I see Bryce walking out of the door and unfortunately Shelby must have already left. After a little small talk in the parking lot I go inside and double check my schedule for tomorrow. Just like every day, a printout of tomorrow's appointments is lying on my desk with a small smiley face in the top right corner. As I mentally take notes, my phone starts to ring.

Vincent: Hey Michelle.

Michelle: Hi Vince. I was calling to let you know that I will be home late tonight. Maria had such a terrible day and I said I would treat her to dinner and a movie.

Vincent: Oh...ok.

Michelle: There are plenty of TV dinners in the freezer. Oh, and leftover spaghetti from yesterday.

Vincent: Sure, I'll figure something out. I hope you two have a good time.

As soon as I hang up, a small part of me feels a little guilt for what I am about to do. I'm sure it's because I've just spoken to Michelle. Scrolling through my phone I select Shelby's name but stop myself before hitting the call button.

Locking up the office I walk out to my car and get inside. Instead of calling Shelby I think I may just stop by and surprise her. She's not expecting me so I can't wait to see her face. Surprisingly, traffic is very light and I make it there in no time. Parking in my usual spot behind the apartment building, I make my way up the stairs to her apartment and ring the bell. A moment later Shelby answers.

"Vincent," she shrieks.

"Hey darling," I reply, smiling at the way her eyes light up.

"What a surprise, what are you doing here?" she asks, stepping aside gesturing for me to follow.

"Well, it looks as though something's come up and I have a few hours until I have to be home so I figured I'd come over and surprise you. It's been so long."

"Oh my god, you are so amazing," she replies, hugging me tight after closing the door. "Are you hungry? I just finished cooking."

"It smells delicious, I am," I say and we both walk into the kitchen.

"It's nothing special, just Chicken Picatta. I hope you'll like it," she says, spooning the sauce over the chicken.

Sitting at her dining table we are lost in conversation. This is what I love about us, we can talk about anything without there being any awkward moments or uncomfortable silence. The food she made is amazing and I am not being bias, she's a wonderful cook.

After dinner, Shelby grabs her phone, syncing it to the wireless speaker on her bookshelf. Joining me on the sofa, we sit there, holding each other close as soft music fills the room

"You really just made my day," she says, her head on my shoulder.

"By showing up at your door?"

"Yes! I never would have expected that," she says moving her head and planting a kiss on my neck.

"I'm glad my surprise worked out. I almost called you beforehand to make sure you'd be home but then decided to just take a chance."

"Well, I'm glad you showed up when you did. After dinner I was supposed to stop by my sister's house," she replies and now I wish I had called.

"Oh I am so sorry, I'm keeping you from your plans I ca-" I begin and she interrupts.

"No, no, no. I already texted her and said something came up. This is exactly where I want to be right now…with you."

With her eyes on me, I place my hand on her cheek, kissing her lips. Wrapping her hands around my neck she maneuvers until she has me pulled down on top of her. We stay like that for the next ten minutes, lost in one another, kissing, making up for lost time.

Next, I get up and she gives me a perplexed look. I take her hand, leading her to the bedroom since the sofa isn't nearly as comfortable. I begin undressing her…slowly, kissing her neck. I've learned it's one of her most sensitive areas and immediately a moan escapes her lips. I continue, my hands finding the zipper of her skirt, pulling it down. Seeing her, in only a bra, panties, garter and thigh highs arouses me even more. To me she is perfection, even if she doesn't believe it. I love every single curve, every supposed flaw, every inch of her.

Asking her to get on the bed, she smiles and I remove my clothes, tossing them in a corner of the room. Joining her on the bed, I remove her bra, my tongue trailing a path from her neck down to her breast. She arches her back in pleasure, her hand in my hair. My lips make their way down her body, unhooking the garter and removing it, along with her panties. Peeling off her stockings, my lips graze the inside of her thigh and out of the corner of my eye, I see she is biting her lip. My lips move up her thigh, reaching her sensitive area and I begin pleasuring her with my tongue. She squirms, whimpering, but lost in pure enjoyment. Within moments she reaches her peak and her moans are driving me wild. I feel her hands grip my shoulders, pulling me up toward her, longing for me. Slowly I bury myself inside her, and a groan escapes my lips. I feel her nails run down my back, her lips on my shoulder. I have been longing to be this close to her, to feel her. It's been two weeks since I've held her in my arms and I wish I never had to leave her side again.

Chapter Fourteen

Vincent

I am so exhausted. A full day of shopping in Manhattan will do that to you, especially with two indecisive women. I stopped counting after the eighth department store and figured we would just be heading out tomorrow to check out the shopping malls. Thankfully, Michelle and Ashley both found dresses they really liked and I must say they look stunning. Michelle chose a classic black evening gown with lace sleeves and a sash at the waist, classic yet beautiful. Ashely chose a knee length gold fitted dress and luckily, she found matching shoes at the same store.

Luke and Ashely thought about bringing Libby along but then opted not to, assuming it would be a very long day. They ended up dropping her off with Ashely's parents before meeting us at our house and I'm sure she's had a great time with them. Ashley's parents have two small dogs and a few cats and Libby really loves animals.

In between shopping, the four of us had a small bite to eat since the women didn't think that having a big meal and trying on dresses went well together. We are on our way back home now and Luke convinced us to go to a Sushi place close to home. I am going to be honest, I have never tried it, nor have the desire to but Ashely assured us that they have other options on the menu.

As soon as we walk in the door, the hostess seats us at a table in the back. I really like the atmosphere, dim lights, traditional decorations. As I look over the menu I see Luke placing X's on a piece of paper.

"What are you doing Luke?" I ask.

"Oh, just marking the sushi rolls we want to order. We don't need the menu anymore," Luke responds and Michelle says she's going to be adventurous and try the sushi.

"Come on Vince," Ashely begins. "Just try it, I'm sure you'll love it."

"Alright, you talked me into it," I say, closing the menu and setting it on the table.

"I'm so proud of you honey," Michelle says, grabbing my hand on the table and holding it.

For a moment I'm shocked. She doesn't normally do this. Actually, come to think of it, she's been a bit more affectionate than usual. She must have something up her sleeve again.

After placing our order, it takes about twenty minutes for our food to arrive. I am actually quite surprised that they bring out an entire wooden bridge with pieces of sushi all over it. I must say, the presentation is beautiful and it's apparent that a lot of hard work has gone into this meal.

Picking up the chopsticks, which by the way I do know how to use, I'm torn on which piece to try. Before the waiter left, he pointed out which roll was which but I can't remember a single one.

"I would try this one first if I were you," Ashley begins. "It's the California roll."

Taking her advice, that is the one I go for and I am actually pleasantly surprised, it tastes delicious. We ordered about ten different rolls and I am proud to say that I tried each and every one of them. After this experience I came to the conclusion that I enjoyed the rolls with the raw fish the most. I suppose it's good to be adventurous sometimes.

On the ride home, Shelby pops into my mind. Well, she's never actually left my mind, I think about her all the time. It's days like these when the guilt eats at me, the days we actually spend together as a family. Obviously, it's not enough for me to end my relationship with Shelby. Even just thinking about it kills me. Some nights when I go to bed and fall asleep next to my wife I feel as if I'm cheating on Shelby, I know it sounds insane.

Finally arriving home we say goodbye to the kids and they get into their car and head to Ashely's parents home to pick up Libby. Walking into house, Michelle and I hang up our coats and she asks if I'd like a cup of coffee. Telling her I'd love one I go into the living room and sit on the sofa, scrolling through the emails on my phone. Michelle joins me about five minutes later handing me a cup, sitting next to me. A moment later, the thought of her holding my hand comes to mind and a part of me wonders if this is her way of telling me that she wants us to be close again. My left hand searches for hers and as soon as we touch, she moves her hand away, leaving me puzzled. I normally just shrug it off but I decide to say something this time.

"Is everything alright Michelle?" I ask and she looks at me.

"What are you talking about Vince, of course everything is alright, why do you ask?'

"You just pulled your hand away," I reply and she rolls her eyes.

"Well, maybe I don't feel like being touched right now," she says and I'm not letting this go.

"All day you were so affectionate, grabbing my hand, kissing my cheek. Why is it every time I try to connect with you, you end up pushing me away?"

"Oh my god Vince, I think you are being a bit dramatic. You know I've never been the cuddly type, why would that change after twenty-six years?"

Knowing that I won't get anywhere with her I just agree and give up. It was wishful thinking that something changed. A few minutes later I notice that she's occupied with her phone so I go upstairs and get ready for bed.

The next morning, I wake up and notice Michelle never came to bed. Her side is untouched and it's not like her at all. Coming downstairs I walk into the living room and she's lying on the couch, sleeping. Walking over to her I tap her shoulder and she opens her eyes.

"What time is it?" she asks, rubbing her eyes.

"It's 8 am," I reply and her eyes widen.

"Oh my god. I must have fallen asleep. I was texting Maria to see if she was feeling better and I guess I nodded off," she begins. "Hey Vince, I want to apologize for last night."

"What do you mean?" I ask, a little surprised.

"Well, for my attitude. I didn't mean it the way I said it. Maybe its menopause. Remember when your mom was a little nuts around my age?"

"Of course," I lie, my mom has always been very even tempered, at least around all of us kids.

Sure, menopause has been known to mess with a woman's hormone levels but this has been going on for a long time. I'm sure it's just another excuse but I will give her the benefit of the doubt, what else can I do.

Shelby

I am at my sister's house getting ready for my work
Christmas Party. I didn't know which dress to wear so I'm
letting Kristi choose for me. She has great taste and has
always been my go to when I feel torn. Sometimes I wish I
could tell her about Vincent and me to ask for advice. Who
am I kidding? I'm sure I wouldn't get her blessing in this
matter. A part of me hates that I have to keep this special
part of my life locked away as if it didn't exist but I guess I
knew what I was getting into beforehand. Things between
Vincent and I have been going great and I've been able to
see him more than before, actually about three times a
week now. Once in a while he will show up for a surprise
visit which always makes me happy.

"Shelby," I hear Kristi shouting from the other room.
"How long do we have to wait to see these dresses?"

"Sorry," I yell, gathering my thoughts and walking into
the living room.

Right now, I am wearing a dark blue evening gown with a
halter top. It's flowy and very comfortable but the cutout
at the bust is quite low.

"Wow, it's gorgeous but you fill that dress a little too
well," Kristi comments, looking directly at my chest.

"Yeah, I was thinking the same thing, too much?" I ask
and she nods.

I walk back into the bedroom and change into the next one, a black classic one strap dress. As soon as I walk out I can tell this is a no from Kristi's expression and I turn around and head back to the bedroom. Well, I have one left. A strapless dark green chiffon evening gown with a sweetheart neckline. I bought this dress about two weeks ago, thinking this is the one I would be wearing but after trying it on at home I wasn't sure. Stepping out in the living room Kristi stands up and gives me a thorough look over.

"Shelby, I love this one, it's beautiful," she says and now I feel much better about my selection.

"Not too revealing with it being strapless?" I ask and she giggles.

"Well, you are always going to have an issue with that because of your size, but you look very classy so I think you'll be able to pull it off. I wish I would have been blessed with at least half of what you have. Anyway, how are you wearing your hair?"

"I was just thinking a low bun with a few strands out in the front," I say and she immediately begins playing with my hair.

About twenty minutes later she finishes and I love what she's done. Instead of a regular bun she placed a loose braid down the left side of my head and stuck the remainder of the braid in a bun, using about twenty bobby pins. After almost killing me with a bottle of hairspray she starts on my makeup. I have to say I am just a bit nervous when she hands me the mirror, I usually don't let anyone do my makeup, not even her. Opening my eyes, I am positively surprised. I look like a 1920's movie star, classically beautiful.

I can't wait to see Vincent's reaction. Thanking my sister for all of her help, I look at the time and realize I have to get ready to go if I don't want to be late. The party is being held at one of the popular hotel's ballrooms and I'm definitely excited. As soon as I walk in I see a big board outside the ballroom with seat assignments. Searching for my name it looks as if our firm is seated together, along with a few names I don't recognize. Then I see her name, Michelle Steele. Oh my god, it never dawned on me that she would accompany him to this party. I have yet to meet her in person and I just hope that everything goes smooth. I just wasn't to turn around and go home.

"Shelby," a voice startles me and I turn around.

"Oh good evening Mr. Preston, Mrs. Preston," I reply.

"It's great to meet you Shelby, you can call me Jessica, I've heard a lot about you and am glad I finally get to meet you," Jessica grabs my arm, basically pulling me into the ballroom.

Jessica Preston is around my age, with blonde hair and blue eyes, very beautiful. She and Bryce actually look like the perfect couple if there is such a thing. Navigating to our table, we find our seats and I am seated between Bryce and Vincent. Jessica asks Bryce to switch seats with her so we can continue our conversation. I learn that she is originally from the Midwest and has been having a difficult time getting used to big city life. Taking a sip of my water, my eyes wander towards the door way and I see him. Instantly my heart skips a beat and I feel myself get weak in the knees. He's wearing a traditional black tuxedo that looks as if it were made for him. A second later I'm pulled out of my little world when I see his wife step next to him. With his hand on her lower back, he leads her to our table and a little part of me dies right there. A simple and probably meaningless gesture, but it hurts anyway.

Vincent shoots me the tiniest little smile and for a moment I forget everything else – until the introductions are made. Mrs. Steele gives me a slight nod with the typical *it's nice to meet you*. It's good that way though, I'd rather not engage in deep conversation with her.

Once everyone has arrived the organizer, Jack, has a few announcements to make and about fifteen minutes later dinner starts to arrive. There is soft music playing in the background and overall the atmosphere is great. After dessert, I feel Michelle's eyes on me and I look her way, giving her an obligatory smile.

"So Shelby," Michelle begins, catching me off guard. "Vince says you've lived in a lot of different places?"

"I have. My father transferred jobs quite a bit so we had the opportunity to travel around the country," I reply, removing the napkin from my lap, placing it next to my plate.

"Did your travels take you overseas at all?" she asks, and right now I wonder where the sudden interest is coming from.

"Unfortunately no," I respond. "I would love to travel to Europe someday though."

"Europe is great. We took a trip a few years back and had a wonderful time," she smiles.

"Mr. Steele mentioned the family taking a vacation there," I respond and Vincent take a sip of his wine. "What was your favorite place to visit?"

"Wow, there are so many. I did enjoy Kiev and Verona," she reminisces. "Australia was great as well."

Our conversation continues and people have gravitated toward the dancefloor. About fifteen minutes later a song gets Michelle's attention.

"Shelby, will you excuse me," she says, her attention on Vincent. "Vince, let's dance. I haven't heard this song in years."

"Of course dear," he responds, giving me a quick glace that almost looks apologetic.

I get up and walk toward Bryce and Jessica who have mingled with a few others and within seconds I'm drawn into the conversation. I can't help but glance toward the dancefloor every so often and what I see is a happy couple. Seeing Vincent and Michelle so close, sets off an uncomfortable feeling inside me. Michelle never felt real to me until today. Obviously, I knew he had a wife, I knew she existed but having her in front of me in the flesh just put things into perspective. She's very nice and nothing like I imagined. What am I doing? I need to get out of here.

Chapter Fifteen

Vincent

When Michelle and I return to our table from the dancefloor I scan the room and can't find Shelby anywhere. As we sit down we are joined by a couple from another law office. I've seen him at court a time or two but we've never had time to actually speak to one another. About ten minutes later I see Shelby walking towards the table. God, she looks gorgeous tonight, a classic beauty. I'm sure this can't be easy for her. This is the first time Shelby and Michelle have met and I must admit, a small part of me was a bit paranoid before getting here, what if Michelle could see right through us?

"Shelby," Bryce's wife Jessica shrieks as she intercepts Shelby before she's able to sit down. "You have to come with me, I need to introduce you to Dominic. He's a friend of ours, a lawyer as well. Come on."

Before Shelby can say a word, Jessica has her by the hand and is dragging her toward her husband and a man that I've never seen before. Watching the scene unfold my pulse begins to quicken. Seeing Shelby interact with another man, smiling and laughing is igniting a side of me I didn't know I had. I have never been the jealous type and to be honest, I have no right to feel this way.

Suddenly John comes walking up and I'm surprised to see him. He had called me earlier to let me know he may not make it to the party since one of his children had come down with the flu.

"Hey Vince, Michelle."

"John, Vince said you weren't going to make it," Michelle says, getting up to give him a hug.

"Well, I wasn't but my wife said I should at least make an appearance. Besides, I want to see if I win the big prize when they hold the drawing."

"Well, you're in luck John, it hasn't started," I reply and he laughs.

"Well Michelle, I would like to say you look absolutely stunning tonight," John smiles. "Vince, do you mind if I steal her for a dance?"

"I don't mind," I say and Michelle gets up letting John lead her toward the crowded dancefloor.

Thinking this may be a good time to go to the bar to get a drink, I get up and see that Shelby is coming back to the table.

"Hey Shelby," I say as she sits next to me.

"Mr. Steele," she replies, almost avoiding eye contact.

"I'm sorry about tonight," I say in a lowered voice.

"What do you mean?" she replies, those eyes staring right through me.

"Well, I'm sure this isn't the most comfortable thing. I'm sorry that I put you in this position."

"No need to apologize. It's not like I didn't know you were married before. I knew I would run into her at one time or another, it's unavoidable," she says.

"I guess you're right," I say and before I can say another word, Bryce and Jessica appear.

The rest of the night goes well. John actually does win the main prize, a three-day cruise to Mexico, lucky for him he showed up. I'm sure his wife will be equally excited.

"Alright guys, I'm out of here. See you at work on Monday," John announces before heading out of the door.

"I think we've about had it as well," Bryce says, putting his arm around Jessica. "Thankfully we booked a room here. I'd hate to make that drive home right now.

"We did the same," Michelle smiles.

"Really? Which room?" Jessica asks.

"304," Michelle replies and Jessica points out that they are on the same floor as we are.

"Shelby, are you staying here as well?" Jessica asks.

"Oh no, I don't live too far from here," Shelby replies, hiding a yawn with her hand. "I'm going to head out now as well. It was really nice meeting all of you. I had a great time."

"Great to finally meet you Shelby," Michelle says. "Vince, why don't you walk Shelby to her car, it's late."

"Oh, Mrs. Steele, that's not necessary, I'm fine," Shelby insists.

"It's no trouble Shelby," I counter and she agrees.

Collecting her things, we make our way out of the ballroom and through the revolving door leading outside the hotel. It's takes a little while to get to her car since she parked on the third level of the parking deck and I'm happy to have accompanied her even though we haven't spoken a world.

"Thank you for walking me to my car Mr. St-, I mean, Vincent," she says with a coy smile.

"Your welcome Shelby, anytime," I say, brushing her hand slightly.

Suddenly her hand envelops mine and feeling her touch is something I have been craving all night. Looking at her she is standing there with her eyes closed, taking in this moment. She opens her eyes and gives me one of her beautiful smiles which warms my heart in an instant. Placing my hand on her cheek she takes a quick glance around the parking lot, making sure no one see us. I know it sounds foolish of me but right at this moment I don't care. I lean forward, kissing her forehead before telling her to drive safe.

Shelby

Even though it is late, the first thing I do when I get home is stand in the shower. I have so many things going through my head right now and in a way, I wish I could just wash the entire night away. All except for that moment at my car, that was truly beautiful. I just don't know what to do. I knew he was married but it was different seeing her in person. I felt guilty. Guilty for touching him, the intimacy we've shared but most of all, guilty for loving him. Tonight was the night I realized that the man I love belongs to someone else and it kills me inside, knowing that I will never have him for myself. What do I do? Do I let him go? It would be the smartest decision, even if it feels like it would tear my heart to shreds.

Waking up the next day I don't feel any better, nor have I come to a decision on how I should proceed. Grabbing my phone off my nightstand I have a message from Vincent. Swiping the screen it reads *Good morning Shelby, I wanted to tell you that you looked absolutely stunning last night and I wish I could have shared a dance with you. I want you to know that you are the first thing on my mind when I wake and the last before I fall asleep.*

Reading the message brings a tear to my eye and I can't stop staring at it. I must have re-read it about ten times before replying. I think this just gave me the answer I needed. There is no way I can leave him. Even if will never be able to walk hand in hand or share a kiss in public, I never want to know what it's like to be without him. I will do my best to enjoy the present and not worry about the future.

When I get to work Monday morning, the sight of Vincent's car already puts a smile on my face. Now I feel ridiculous for even entertaining the idea of leaving him, there's no way I could. I'm sure I may go through the ruts from time to time, but I'll just have to push through. As I walk into the office I see Vincent standing at my desk, placing a folder next to my keyboard.

"Good morning Mr. Steele," I say in a cheerful tone. "What do you have for me?"

"Good morning Shelby," he responds with a smile. "Just a few dates for upcoming seminars. Would you please pencil them into my schedule?"

"Oh of course, Sir. Are you going anywhere interesting?" I ask, since I assume seminars are usually out of town.

He leans in close and whispers, "Are we going anywhere interesting you mean…and yes, I think you may enjoy the location."

My eyes widen and I can't get a word out. Thankfully I don't to have since Vincent returns to his office and John walks out of his. Opening the folder, it looks like there are two seminars. One in Las Vegas and the other in Boston. Looking at the dates I notice that the Vegas one is coming up very soon, from the 13th to the 16th of January. I am so excited but have a few questions for him so I grab my phone and send him a message. Responding, he says we can go over details when he comes by my place later.

I notice the Boston seminar is in March, the weekend of Hayley's birthday. I have never missed one since she was born, but with her getting older I'm sure she won't be too disappointed. I'll just make sure to do something special with her the weekend before.

Later that afternoon when Vincent arrives at my apartment, I fall into his arms as soon as he comes through the door. Shutting the door with his foot he grabs me by the waist, and moments later he has me pushed against the wall, tearing my blouse off me. I find his belt, unhooking it and pull it out of the loops. As soon as my hand finds him, he starts to groan and I gently pull on his lower lip with my teeth.

About twenty minutes later, we are still in each other's arms, half clothed, trying to catch our breath.

"Wow," he comments. "At least I was able to shut the door. That was amazing."

"Sorry, lust and desire took over I guess," I giggle, planting a kiss on his neck.

"Don't apologize, I'm not sure I've ever felt this wanted in my life," he says and I give him a puzzled expression.

"Oh so you mean to say all the other times I failed to bring my point across?" I reply in a joking tone.

"Definitely not," he says, kissing my lips. "You always make me feel wanted."

After getting dressed he brings up the subject of the seminars.

"So, you had some questions about the seminars?"

"Oh yes, let's go sit down. Do you want anything to drink?" I ask.

"Water is fine," he replies and I walk into the kitchen and return with two glasses of water.

"Okay, so do you think it will be strange if we both take that Friday off?" I begin.

"No, I don't think it will be a problem," he explains.

"What if John or Bryce want to join you?" I counter.

"They won't, John has plans that weekend and I just know that Bryce won't be interested."

"Okay, so when should I get my plane ticket?"

"I'm taking care of that. You just have to show up at the airport. I'll have your flight leave a couple of hours after mine but I will be waiting for you at the airport."

"Wow, you've thought of everything," I smile and he plants a kiss on my cheek.

Chapter Sixteen

Vincent

It's December 31st and my wife and I are invited to Paula's annual New Years Eve Bash. This is our first year attending and I know Michelle has really been looking forward to it since most of her book club will be there. I don't know very much about Paula except for that she is divorced and has a teenaged daughter. If I remember correctly she may be dating a plastic surgeon, but I could be wrong.

Michelle and I haven't gotten into anymore arguments lately but now it seems as if we barely say five words to one another. I guess it's not much different than before, maybe I just notice it more now. It's a different story when we are around people though, then she likes to pretend we are in our honeymoon phase and to be honest I'm getting a little sick of it. Let's pretend we live this perfect life because it's so important to impress others. Don't get me wrong, I would never cause a scene but I also don't believe we have to be overly affectionate to each other if it's all a lie anyway.

Sitting downstairs I'm waiting for Michelle to finish getting dressed. A moment later my phone chimes and I take it out of my back pocket. Assuming the message is from Shelby, I waste no time opening the message *Hey Vincent, just wanted to say hi and hope you have a good time at the party. I wish I could give you a New Years kiss*

145

at midnight, just know I will be thinking of you. Staring at the screen I take a deep breath before I reply. I would love nothing more than to spend that moment with her, someone that actually enjoys my company and makes me feel wanted.

"Alright Vince, ready?" Michelle asks as she steps into the room.

I nod and place my phone back into my pocket. Before we walk out of the door I run back into the kitchen to grab the bottle of wine we bought as a gift for the hostess. We arrive within fifteen minutes and the party is already in full swing. Paula hired everything from servers to a DJ. I knew this was a big event, just how big I had no idea. After being introduced to Ted, Paula's boyfriend, she and Michelle make their way to the other room and join a group of women in conversation.

"So Vince," Ted begins. "How's business?"

"It's pretty good, steady," I reply. "I'm sure you stay quite busy yourself."

"Oh God," he replies, smiling. "I can't say I'm hurting. Women always want to look like the models in the magazines so they come to me to achieve the look."

"Do you enjoy what you do?" I ask.

"I used to. When I started I thought I was really making a difference, helping people. I remember a case years ago of a young woman who had significantly uneven breasts. She was so embarrassed that she shied away from relationships."

146

"Oh wow, that is really sad."

"It was. She had a hard time letting me take a look at her, she said growing up she was teased by other girls in school. That was a surgery I was really looking forward to, because I knew I could make a difference."

"I'm sure she was very happy with the result."

"Oh, she was. Once I removed the bandages at her post op appointment her face lit up and she cried for joy."

"That is a wonderful reward, knowing that you were able to help her," I comment.

"Definitely, but nowadays things have changed. I see less of these cases and more botox or unrealistic beauty goals. Everyone is looking for the full lips, high cheekbones, abnormally large breasts…but hell, it keeps me in business I guess," Ted raises his eyebrows before taking a sip of his whisky.

About an hour later Michelle comes to find me and pulls me into the living area. It's close to midnight and everyone is focused on the TV, waiting for the ball to drop. Twenty second later, it drops and you can hear the fireworks outside. Michelle grabs me and kisses me like she hasn't in years.

"Oh my god, you two are so adorable," Paula comments. "After so many years too."

Little does she know.

We stay for about another two hours before saying our goodbyes and heading home. On the ride home, Michelle fills me in on all of the gossip she heard at the party and I must admit, some of the stories are pretty funny.

Once at home we head upstairs and I go to the bathroom to brush my teeth. After changing into my pajama bottoms I get into bed and Michelle comes out of the bathroom in her robe. Walking toward my side of the bed, she leans down to kiss me and a moment later she straddles me. I'm taken aback by her actually initiating the intimacy.

I'm awoken by the light coming through a break in the curtains. Lying in bed I look over at Michelle, peacefully sleeping. Staring back at the ceiling I exhale deeply. Why do I feel as if I am living with a stranger? Don't get me wrong, the sex was great but right now I am overcome with a feeling of emptiness, a void that seems to be getting bigger and bigger. For a moment I wonder if it would be better to end my relationship with Shelby. In the beginning I told myself that it was actually a good thing, I had my outlet and there was less tension between Michelle and I. The logical side of me knows that there is no way I can even attempt to fix my marriage while I'm involved with another woman, but do I really want to fix it?

Shelby

These are the moment I hate being the other woman. Not
being able to spend holidays or special occasions with the
man that is so close to my heart and knowing someone else
is. I wanted nothing more than to take Vincent into my
arms, hold him tight and kiss him as we rung in the new
year. Instead I spent it with a group of friends at a bar,
talking about the single life. I knew what I signed up for,
it's not like it was some sort of surprise, but I still have
moments that feel as if a knife is being driven right into my
heart. On a lighter note, I can't wait for our trip to Las
Vegas. I know we still won't be able to walk around hand
in hand since I'm sure there will be other Lawyers there
that Vincent knows but at least I will be able to fall asleep
next to him.

I'm spending New Year's Day cleaning out my apartment
to get rid of things I no longer need. Why does one person
have eight dinner plates? Totally unnecessary, I think four
will be more than enough. As I am immersed in my
cleaning, my phone rings and I get up to see who it is. To
my surprise I see Vincent's name on the caller ID. It's very
rare that we ever get to actually talk on the phone.

Shelby: Hello?

Vincent: Hey Shelby, happy new year.

Shelby: Happy new year to you too. I'm surprised that you're
actually calling me.

Vincent: I'm on my way to my family's house. I just wanted to hear your voice.

Shelby: You are so sweet. I miss you.

Vincent: I miss you too, Shelby. I wish I coul- Oh, sorry I have to go, have another call. I will see at work tomorrow.

Shelby: Can't wait. Goodbye Vincent.

Vincent: Bye Shelby.

Hearing his voice, knowing he was thinking about me sends a big smile to my lips. I may sound crazy but there is something about his voice that makes me forget everything. Even if I wanted to quit this man I don't think I could.

Today is January 12th and I am so excited to fly to Vegas tomorrow. I'm still in disbelief that I will get to spend the next few days with Vincent. Having him to myself for a few days is something I've only ever dreamed of. Looking at the clock it's only 2 pm and I feel as if this day will never end. Vincent and John are at court today so the office has been very quiet.

"Hey Shelby, can I ask you a favor?" Bryce says as he comes walking up to my desk.

"Of course, Mr. Parker," I reply.

"I've been trying to locate Mr. Robbins file for the last two days. I know I had it last but I've already searched my entire office, could you see if you can find it?"

"Right away," I smile, getting up from my desk and checking the file cabinet.

A moment later I recall seeing that file on Vincent's desk yesterday so I make my way to his office to check if it's still there. Vincent keeps his desk very tidy so it's never hard to find anything. Just as I thought, there it is. Picking it up I turn around to leave the office when I see Vincent standing in the doorway.

"Hello Shelby," Vincent says with a smile.

"Mr. Steele, how did things go today?"

"Wonderful," he replies, walking towards me setting his briefcase on the desk.

"That's great," I say, looking into his eyes.

"I can't wait for tomorrow, it can't come soon enough," he whispers, brushing my arm ever so slightly.

"Me too," I reply, biting my lip. "I better go, Bryce was looking for this file."

"You're probably right," he chuckles and I walk out of the office.

I swear if we were alone I know I would have ended up on that desk again. I could see it in his eyes, the longing, the want. It seems as if we can never get enough of one another, I've never felt that way about anyone.

When I get home, I get my suitcase out of the spare room and put it on my bed. Standing in front of my closet I have a hard time deciding what to pack. It's really just for two days so I need to make sure I don't overpack. After twenty minutes I finally finish packing and a part of me wonders why I decided to add a little black dress. It's not like we can really go out to dinner together. The possibility of someone seeing us is too great. Oh well, better to be overprepared.

I spend my evening on the couch, binge watching an ER drama. I don't watch a lot of TV but this show has me hooked. Picking up my phone from the side table I notice that I have a message from Vincent. He always messages me goodnight and I think it's the sweetest thing. I notice that he actually sent it a half hour ago so I'm sure he's fast asleep by now but I still send a reply. Grabbing the blanket from the top of the couch, I lie down and continue watching my show until I fall asleep.

Chapter Seventeen

Vincent

Sitting at McCarran International Airport in Las Vegas, I'm anxiously awaiting Shelby's arrival. Looking at the board, her flight is enroute and should be landing in about thirty minutes. A shuttle will be taking us to our hotel on the strip, where I reserved two rooms, side by side, with an adjoining door. Since the seminar is being held in the same hotel I'm quite certain most of the attendees will be staying here as well and I'm bound to run into people that I know.

I'm on my second cup of coffee and have already read the entire paper so I figure this may be a good time to catch up on some emails. Pulling out my phone I get to work and actually come across an email from John that requires my attention, well, it could wait until I return but since I'm just sitting here I may as well get it out of the way now.

Checking my watch, I notice this last half hour has flown by very quickly. Walking over to the board and discarding my paper cup, I see that Shelby's flight has landed. After collecting my things, I make my way to the arrivals area. As I wait, I watch the first group of passengers walk past me, some being met by loved ones. Smirking I imagine pulling Shelby in for an embrace, kissing her passionately. Unfortunately, that can't happen. Suddenly a thought hits me, I hope Shelby is aware of that. How I would hate to be forced to turn her down, I'm sure she would be hurt. I look up and see those mesmerizing green eyes and that beautiful smile and I can't help to smile myself. Never mind a hug, my face is already giving everything away.

"Good evening Mr. Steele," Shelby says reaching out her hand, how did I ever doubt her?

"Ms. Hunter, how was your flight?"

"Very relaxing actually. I've never flown first class before," she replies.

"I'm happy you enjoyed the experience. Let's collect your luggage, shall we?" I say as we head to baggage claim.

Luckily, we don't have to wait very long, her suitcase is one of the first on the conveyer belt. It isn't a long ride from the airport to our hotel. I've attended several seminars here over the years and am quite familiar with this city. Once the shuttle comes to a stop, I see Shelby's eyes widen, yes, the hotel is definitely a magnificent sight. As we walk up to the reception desk, the clerk greets us with a smile.

"Good evening, welcome to Caesar's Palace. How may I help you?"

"Good evening. Yes, we have a reservation for two rooms under the names of Steele and Hunter," I reply and Shelby lifts an eyebrow. I may have failed to mention that I booked separate rooms.

"Yes sir, one moment please," the clerk replies, typing away on his keyboard.

Next, he hands us each a form, asking for a signature and after going over all of the amenities and features he hands us each a keycard. As we walk towards the elevators I can see Shelby's jaw drop, admiring every detail. Setting my luggage down, I press the button next to the elevator door. Once the doors open, we step inside and I'm relieved that it's just the two of us. I press the button to take us to the sixteenth floor and the doors close.

"Two rooms?" Shelby asks, curiously and I knew it would come up.

"Yes. I had to be sure just in case an acquaintance is staying on our floor," I start. "There's an adjoining door."

"That's smart," she counters. "You know, sometimes it slips my mind."

"What?"

"That you're not really mine," she says, lowering her head slightly.

"Hey," I say, my fingers on her chin, raising it up so I'm staring into her eyes. "I am yours. My heart belongs to you."

Not even a second later, her frown disappears and she can't help but smile. I lean in, kissing her lips and she immediately responds, wrapping her hand around my neck, pulling me closer. Sadly, the kiss is cut short by the chime of the elevator letting us know we reached our floor.

Navigating our way down the hallway, I am very happy that we aren't near the elevators, but tucked away in a corner. We each stand in front of our doors and she giggles, making me burst out laughing. Taking the card out of her pocket, she swipes it and presses down on the handle.

"Mr. Steele," she says.

"Ms. Hunter," I reply with a smile and then she disappears into her room.

Unlocking my own door, I walk in and turn on the light, taking a look around. Massive King-sized bed with a plush headboard, a dark blue L-shaped sofa, a desk and a round table with two large empire style chairs. Setting my briefcase on the desk I walk toward the adjoining door to Shelby's room and unlock my side, knocking slightly. Hearing the click of the lock on her side, she opens the door.

"Mr. Steele. What a surprise, how can I help you?" Shelby asks, standing there in her skirt, blouse and heels, biting that lower lip.

"I don't even have a comeback," I admit. "Isn't that sad?"

"Not at all," she smiles. "Are you going to ask me to come into you room?"

Chuckling, I grab her arm, pulling her close to me, giving her the kiss she deserved when she walked up to me at the airport. My lips travel down her neck and my fingers peel away the collar of her blouse, exposing the strap of her bra. Moving her head back, she lets out a slight moan and then my phone start to ring.

"Damn it," I curse.

"Don't worry, go ahead," she says and I walk over to the desk, retrieving the phone and see it's Michelle.

Shelby

I must admit, it's just a little uncomfortable being in the room while Vincent has a conversation with his wife. I'm sure it won't be the only time. I can tell it's awkward for him as well, I see it in his demeanor. Since it seems as if this isn't going to be a quick conversation I walk back into my room and figure it would be a good time to unpack my suitcase. About five minutes later, Vincent walks into my room, apologizing.

"Don't worry Vincent, I understand. You don't have to apologize," I say, walking up to him and holding him tight.

"You are incredible. I'm still sorry that I kind of ruined that moment we had there," he says kissing my forehead.

"I'm sure there will be many more," I say optimistically, making his eyes light up.

"Are you hungry?" he asks.

"Starving," I reply.

"What do you think about room service?"

"Sound good to me," I smile and he grabs my hand, leading me back into his room.

Looking at the menu we each choose an entrée and relax on the sofa while we wait. A few minutes later Vincent walks over to the TV, switches it on and searches for the music station. After browsing the categories, he hits play and it seems as if he's chosen the love song station, which totally works for me. I am a hopeless romantic at heart. About ten minutes later, there is a knock on the door and Vincent gets up to answer. The attendant enters with a cart and sets our plates on the round table in the room, along with a bottle of wine, glasses and two waters. After tipping the attendant, Vincent closes the door and walks toward the table as I get up to meet him there.

"Sorry, I didn't think tequila would go well with the meal," he jokes.

"You remembered," I laugh. "I suppose you don't want to see if my clothes will fall off."

"Oh, my love, they most certainly will."

The food is exceptional and I'm glad it wasn't overly filling. For not being a wine lover, I will say, this one is very smooth and before I return to the sofa, I pour myself another glass. As I sit down, Vincent's hand is on my legs, pulling them up and removing my shoes. Next, he starts massaging my calves, which are now in his lap.

"Oh my god, that feels so amazing," I say, propped up with a pillow, taking a sip of my wine.

"You're amazing," he replies. "Amazing, beautiful, warm, kind. You are my treasure."

"Wow," I say, eyes widened. "I feel my cheeks burning. How is it possible that you still make me blush?"

"I love doing that to you, the effect my words have. It's the utmost compliment."

"I wish I could freeze time and we'd never had to go back to New York, just you and me together," I say, taking a deep breath as his eyes focus on mine. "I love you Vincent."

"Shelby, I-"

"No, before you say anything, I want you to know I don't expect you to say it back. I know you can't, even if you wanted to. I just wanted to let you know that I truly care about you Vincent. I really mean it."

"I don't know what to say. I feel as if my life began the day you appeared. You are so special to me and I care about you deeply, Shelby. A piece of my heart will always be yours," he replies and that trumps any *I love you too.*

"You melt me," I say, completely enamored with him.

"Hey," he says, moving my legs from his lap and taking the glass of wine out of my hand and setting in on the table. "I have an idea."

"What?" I ask, curiosity almost killing me.

"You and I are going to share a dance."

"Here?"

"Yes!"

"Should I put on my shoes?" I ask, feeling a little silly.

"Most definitely," he replies with a smile.

Vincent hands me my heels before getting up and I slip into them before he grabs my hands, leading me to a spacious area of the room. Taking my hand in his, his other finds my waist, pulling me close. My right hand wraps around the back of his neck and he starts to lead, swaying me back and forth. It's at that moment I actually take note of the song playing in the background, WONDERFUL TONIGHT by ERIC CLAPTON. I haven't heard that song in years.

"Vincent, I think this is the most beautiful thing anyone has ever done for me," I say and he smiles.

"Well, I really would have loved to dance with you at the Christmas Party but that was impossible. I honestly prefer this, just you and me."

He's right, I wouldn't trade this moment for anything. This may have been the most innocent thing we've ever done, yet it feels so intimate at the same time. At this point I'm not sure how many songs have come and gone but there is no place I'd rather be than wrapped in his arms with my head on his shoulder. Suddenly one of his hands leaves my waist and I feel his fingers move my hair to one side. I lift my head and feel his lips gently trailing kisses from the bottom of my neck up to my jawline. Closing my eyes, the sensation of his tongue against my skin makes my heart pound and blindly, my hand searches for his face, guiding him to my lips. Within seconds my tongue invades his mouth and I feel him groan which turns me on even more. His fingers fumble with the buttons of my blouse and when he can't undo them he steps back for a moment to inspect.

"They are just for style," I tease as I find the seam of it and pull it over my head.

"Glad you told me, otherwise I may have ripped it off," he smiles as his hands move to the zipper on the back of my skirt, pulling it down and letting it fall to the floor. I'm left standing in a black lacy bra, a thong, thigh highs and heels.

"You are so beautiful," he groans, his eyes reflecting pure happiness.

I move my hands to start on his shirt but he grabs them and I cock my head to the side, wondering why he's stopping me. He tells me he has to go get something but he will be right back. When he leaves the room I rack my brain, wondering what he might be returning with. Removing my heels and stockings I sit on the bed, my back against the headboard and close my eyes, replaying the moment we first locked eyes in his office. About two minutes later I hear the door open and Vincent returns with a bucket of ice.

"Okay, don't laugh," he begins. "I've always wanted to do this."

"That is so hot," I reply, knowing exactly what he wants to do with the ice cubes.

"Phew," he exhales walking toward the bed, setting the bucket on the nightstand. "I wasn't sure how you'd react to be quite honest. May I blindfold you?"

"With your tie?" I counter, licking my lip.

"Yes. I even brought your favorite one," he smiles.

"Well, how can I say no to that," I smile and he walks to the closet, retrieving the blue stiped tie that I love.

Tying it in a knot at the back of my head. Being robbed of my sight I now rely on my other senses which is new for me. I may have done this to him but I've never experienced it for myself. Feeling him get off the bed, I slide down a little so I am laying down with my head on the pillow. The music is still playing but I can still hear the rustling sound of Vincent removing his shirt. The metal sound of his belt buckle sends a grin to my lips and seconds later I feel him on the bed with me. I feel his hands move between the bed and my back, unhooking my bra and removing it. I know that he is reaching for the ice right now, his watch hitting the metal bucket was a giveaway and even though I was anticipating his next step, it still surprised me. Feeling the ice cube run down my breast makes me arch my back immediately. He stops at my nipple, moving the ice in circles around it. I can feel the water run down my breast as it begins to melt against the heat of my skin. Using his free hand, he pulls my thong off entirely and runs his hand up my thigh. Moving my head back, I let out a moan and now his hand is replaced by the ice cube. Running it up and down my inner thigh, I feel his lips caress my left hip, slowly moving across, ending on the right side. My heart is pounding, my breathing labored, all I want is for him to extinguish this fire he started inside me.

"Vincent," I breathe.

"Yes, my love," he counters, before moving his mouth to my breasts.

163

"I want you," I plead and I feel him smile against my skin. "Now!"

Removing the tie from my eyes, I pull him onto me and we engage in the most lustful, wanting kiss we have ever shared. Once he drives into me it doesn't take long to find release, it's been building inside since I saw his smile at the airport. He continues sending me over the edge and tonight it really does feel like he is mine.

Chapter Eighteen

Vincent

I'm awoken by the light of dawn creeping though the curtains of our room. Turning toward Shelby I see the lines of her beautiful body. The sheet is low, exposing the small of her back. With that image and the thought of what transpired last night, I immediately find myself aroused. I crave her, wanting her again, but don't want to wake her.

Moving closer, I drape my arm around her waist and close my eyes. Suddenly, I feel her hand reach behind her, brushing my hip, making its way to my shaft. Instinctively I move closer, running my hand up her hip and down across her stomach. Circling her belly button with a fingertip I make my way lower as her hand continues stroking me up and down. Finding her aroused and longing for my touch, she moves her head, searching for my lips as I lift her thigh, giving me access to her. As soon as I enter her, moans of pleasure fill the room. Sliding my hand back down I begin stimulating her further with my fingers and she pushes back softly, but with some unspoken urgency. My hand moves up, sliding across her body, up over her back and shoulders, finding her breast and squeezing lightly. I continue caressing her until my hand tangles in her hair. My slow strokes come to a halt and she realizes that I'm ready to orgasm but I want this moment to last longer. She reaches back once more and grabs my hip, simultaneously pulling me into her, thrusting her hips back, burying me inside her. The entirety of the movement catches me off guard and I begin thrusting harder. When I can't hold back, I feel myself release, slowly, as my lips caress her back and shoulder. For a moment I hold her close to me, exactly the way we are.

Stealing one more kiss from those beautiful lips I get up and walk toward the shower. Once the water is hot, I step in and begin to daydream that possibly one day we would be able to share our lives together. Even though the glass is covered in fog I notice a shadow cross before the door is pulled open. Shelby steps in, giving me a smile with a look in her eye that drives me wild. A moment later, she looks down and sees that I am still somewhat erect. Placing both hands on my chest she slowly slides down, sinking to her knees, taking me into her mouth, looking up at me in adoration. My head falls back and I find myself lost. Lost in this moment, lost in her.

It's 2 pm and I have about two more hours to go before the seminar is finished for the day. To tell the truth, I'm not gaining anything and the only reason I am attending is for Shelby and I to spend some time together, away from New York. I have run into a few familiar faces and it's been great catching up. Some I haven't seen in over fifteen years and wouldn't have recognized them if they hadn't approached me.

Currently we have a ten-minute break and I would love nothing more than to go up to my room to see Shelby but it's definitely not enough time. Then I wonder, would it be a big deal if I just leave early? No one would care, heck, this room is filled with so many people that I'm sure no one would notice. I get up from my seat and make my way towards the double doors leading out of the ballroom. Not even halfway there I hear a voice call my name.

"Vincent Steele?"

Turning around I see a face I haven't seen since graduating law school.

"Bob Davis," I say. "What a surprise, how have you been?"

"Doing great. I never thought I'd see you again. We never end up at the same events. How's the family?"

"Everyone's great. Our boy's have children of their own now. They both live fairly close so we get to see them quite a bit."

"How many grands do you have?" he inquires.

"Two. Libby and Jackson. How about you?"

"Six," he grins. "There's a set of twins in there as well. Are you still in New York?"

"I am. Same area too. Where did you end up?"

"Right here in lovely Vegas," he says stretching his arms out. "Can't say I'm hurting for business either. We keep very busy. Hey, what do you say we grab dinner tonight, you know, catch up."

"Oh I can't," I begin. "I hav-"

I'm interrupted by the speaker announcing his return and asking us to take our seats. Well, I suppose there goes my idea leaving early.

"Vince, I'll come find you once it's over. Don't take off," Bob smiles and I need to figure out how to get out of this one.

These last two hours seem to last an eternity and at this point, I really can't wait to get out of here. The gentleman next to me has already fallen asleep. After speaking with him earlier today I was surprised to find out that he is still practicing law at age seventy-five. At that age, I would hope that I would be well into retirement. Before the dismissal, the organizer goes over a quick rundown of tomorrows events and once he finishes I make my way to the door. Not even ten seconds later, Bob finds me again.

"So what do you say, there will be a group of us. Harry Collier and Chris Richter will be joining us as well."

"Bob, I would really love to but I already have plans for tonight. How about tomorrow over lunch?" I offer and he agrees.

168

Shelby

Awaiting his return, I lie there, my eyes focused on the door. Within seconds I hear the click of the keycard and my pulse quickens. He steps into the room and moments later his eyes meet mine as he starts to remove his tie, wearing that devilish smile. I get up, meeting him halfway and wrapping my arms around him.

"I've missed you," he says in between kisses.

"I missed you too," I reply. "How was the seminar?"

"Quite boring to tell the truth. I ran into a few people I know. One of them was someone I haven't seen since law school and he was very persistent on me joining him for dinner tonight but luckily I got out of it."

"Well, if you weren't able to I understand," I reply smiling.

"No. This weekend is about you and I. Nothing is going to come between that. How would you like to go out to dinner tonight?"

"Do you think that will be alright?" I say and he gives me a perplexed expression.

"Why wouldn't it be?"

"Well I just figured you wouldn't want to chance anyone seeing us together," I reply and he pulls me back into his arms.

"Don't worry. I was thinking of taking you to a restaurant away from the strip. I'm sure most people will be staying around this area especially on a Saturday night with all the entertainment on one street."

After learning that the restaurant is more on the upscale side I am so happy that I decided to bring along my dress. I may freeze my butt off but at least I will look good. Walking through the adjoining door I walk to my closet, grabbing my dress and placing it on the bed. As I put it on I am having trouble pulling the zipper all the way up in the back. Right now I am happy that Vincent is in the shower, if he saw me twisting and leaning back trying to reach the zipper I'm sure he would burst out laughing. At least all of my effort wasn't for nothing, I got it zipped up. Walking into the bathroom of my room I reapply my makeup and brush my hair. As I lay the brush down I can feel Vincent stand behind me and I turn around.

"Wow. You look gorgeous Shelby," he comments, eyes focused on my bust.

"Well, I like the look you have going there too with the towel around your waist," I smile.

"Oh yeah. Will you take me out like this?" he jokes.

"I prefer that look for my eyes only," I reply and he kisses my forehead before returning to his room to get ready.

It probably seems ridiculous but when I leave I exit through my room door, better safe than sorry. Shutting the door behind me, Vincent steps out of his and I'm blown away. He's wearing black pants and a black dress shirt which is a look I haven't seen before, but it suits him so well.

"You look amazing," I say quietly. "Wow."

"I'm glad you like it. I figured I would match your dress."

In the elevator we wait to reach the bottom floor and on the way down a few other people get on. I suppose we won't be sharing any kisses here this time. As we step out of the elevator Vincent says he already called for a taxi and it should be here shortly. Walking past the front desk I hear someone call Vincent name and for a moment I freeze.

"Hey Vince, heading out?"

"We are actually," he replies as the man looks at me with questionable eyes, waiting on an introduction.

"Hello, my name is Bob Davis and you are?" he asks as he shakes my hand, alright Shelby, quick on your feet.

"My name is Kristi Hunter, I'm a paralegal aspiring to become a lawyer one day. That is, if I make it into law school," I say with a smile, it's the best I could come up with.

"Future lawyer, that's great. Do you work for Vince?" Bob asks.

"I do, yes. I know technically I probably shouldn't be attending this seminar but since Mr. Steele's partner wasn't able to make it, he offered that I could take his slot, thinking it could be a great learning experience."

"That is smart. Why let the slot go to waste?" Bob starts. "You weren't sitting with Vince were you? I think I would have noticed you."

"No I wasn't. I was sitting near the exit in the last row in case I had to get up and take a phone call. I have a six-month-old back at home and my fiancé is playing Mr. Mom. Luckily it seems as if he has everything under control."

"I have a four-month-old granddaughter," Bob gushes. "Cherish every moment, they go by fast."

"I second that," Vincent says. "I sometimes can't believe that my children have kids of their own."

"Well Vince," Bob says, slapping him on the back. "What can we say, we are old now. Anyway, sorry I'm probably keeping you. Have a great night and it was wonderful to meet you Kristi."

"You as well Mr. Davis. Enjoy your evening," I reply shaking hand.

"Alright, goodbye Bob. See you tomorrow," Vincent says before we walk outside to find out taxi.

Once in the car Vincent has a look of relief on his face and he turns towards me giving me an funny look.

"Kristi huh?"

"Well, I figured it's best to give him a different name."

"How did you come up with that so fast?" he asks.

"It's just the first thing that popped into my head that didn't sound too ridiculous."

"To be quite honest, it was perfect," Vincent chuckles. "Let's just hope he doesn't go searching for you tomorrow."

"Well, you can just say that I got food poisoning and unfortunately I didn't feel well enough to attend the rest of the seminar," I respond and Vincent shakes his head laughing.

"You definitely could be a lawyer, you are so believable even though the entire thing is a lie."

"Maybe one day," I reply with a smile.

Chapter Nineteen

Vincent

Our time in Las Vegas is something I know I will remember the rest of my life. Falling asleep with Shelby in my arms was an indescribable feeling, a feeling I know I will miss. I am already looking forward to Boston, it can't come soon enough. I would have loved to take her out for a tour of the town but it would have been too risky. I know she explored a few areas while I was engaged in the seminar but I would have loved to share those moments with her. Looking at my watch, I have ten minutes before I board my flight. It's a six-hour trip, direct flight. Shelby is already about halfway to New York by now.

Reflecting on our time spent together, one moment stands out. It's the moment she confessed that she loved me. I will admit I was taken aback by it at the time and wasn't exactly sure how to respond. Yes, I care for her, deeply. I adore her, I treasure her, but do I love her?

Good Afternoon Ladies and Gentlemen. We are now inviting our First-Class passengers on board. Please have your ID and boarding pass ready.

Grabbing my briefcase, I get up and stand in line, well it's not much of a line actually, I only have two people ahead o me. After the attendant checks my boarding pass I walk down the long hall leading to the plane. Judging from the waiting area I believe this flight will have many empty seats. I have a window seat and I'm keeping my fingers crossed that the seat next to me remains unoccupied. On the way here, I had a woman sitting next to me that wouldn't stop talking. Even after pulling out a book, insinuating that I would like to read, she kept at it. I really believe I knew her entire life story within the fist fifteen minutes. When she started asking questions about my life that's when my answers became abrupt and after a while she caught on that I wasn't much of a talker.

Ladies and Gentlemen, we welcome you on board flight 1611 with service from Las Vegas to New York. We are currently third in line for takeoff and are expected to be in the air in approximately seven minutes time. We ask that you please fasten your seatbelts at this time and secure all baggage underneath your seat or in the overhead compartments. We also ask that your seats and table trays are in the upright position. Please turn off all personal electronic devices, including laptops and cell phones. Smoking is prohibited for the duration of this flight. We hope you enjoy your flight.

I lucked out, no one next to me. Turning off my cell phone I place it into my pocket and fasten my seatbelt. I think I will take a much needed nap during this flight.

I'm awoken by the sound of another announcement blaring over the speakers and I'm surprised to learn we are getting ready to land. I slept the entire flight and it feels as if I just nodded off maybe ten minutes ago.

Collecting my suitcase, I make my way to the parking garage and get into my car. It's already 9 pm so traffic shouldn't be bad at all but the drive will still take about forty-five minutes. Before I start the car, I power my phone back on and a message notification appears on my screen *Vincent, I've made it home. Thank you so much for an amazing weekend together. I will miss you tonight and can't wait to see you in the morning xoxo.*

I smile immediately. Before she boarded her flight, I asked her to message me so I would know she made it home safe. Once I reply, letting her know I'm on my way home, I start the car and head home.

Unlocking the front door, I notice the house is dark and very quiet so I'm sure Michelle has already gone to bed. I decide to leave my luggage in the Foyer off to the side to reduce unnecessary noise. Quietly opening the bedroom door, I slip inside and make my way to the bathroom to brush my teeth before heading to bed and falling asleep.

The sound of my alarm pulls me out of my dreams and I blindly reach for the snooze button, but instead, knock the alarm clock off the nightstand. Well done Vincent! Getting up I retrieve it off the floor and turn it off.

"Good morning Vince," Michelle yawns. "I didn't even hear you come in last night."

"Good morning," I say, "It was really late."

"You should have booked an earlier flight."

"You're right. I didn't account for the time difference," I reply.

That was about all of the conversation we had this morning, granted, it's early and Michelle has never been much of a morning person. She did offer to make me breakfast which was sweet of her and she surprised me with waffles. These are the moments I feel guilt ridden.

176

The moments I look at her, knowing she has no idea that I am living this double life, betraying our vows, betraying her. Yet, I can't get myself to end things with Shelby. She makes me feel complete and it's a feeling I have been missing for many years.

Shelby

I must admit, I had a tough time finding sleep last night. After just two days I got so used to drifting off in Vincent's arms, and it made me miss him terribly. Well, there's no use being too sad about it, these moment's will be very rare and I know that.

Filling the coffee maker with water I hear the front door of the office open and I turn around seeing Vincent's face.

"Good morning Mr. Steele. How was the seminar," I ask with a smile.

"Good morning Shelby. It was wonderful. Thank you for asking."

"Of course," I respond. "I will have your files pulled in just a few minutes and I will bring them to your office."

"Perfect," he says before disappearing into his office.

It's already 2 pm and I'm working on a few things John dropped off earlier when the phone rings.

"Steele and Baker, this is Shelby Hunter, how may I help you?"

"Well," a voice I immediately recognize begins. "You can help me by stopping by my office if you have a moment."

"Right away sir," I reply, unable to hide the grin on my lips.

I walk into Vincent's office and he asks me to shut the door. Coming towards me he takes me into his arms, kissing my forehead.

"I've been wanting to do this all morning," he exhales, pulling me even closer.

For a moment we stand there, exactly like that. No words spoken, no words needed. Whenever I'm in his arms, everything seems perfect, or as close to perfection as it can get.

Instead of going home, I head to Kristi's for dinner. It's been a little while since we've seen each other so I'm definitely overdue for a visit. Normally Vincent comes by on Mondays but with him being out of town all weekend, it would be hard to justify working late today and I completely understand that.

"Shelby! God, I feel like I haven't seen you in weeks!" Kristi says, pulling me in for a hug. "I just figured we'd see more of you being single."

"Sorry, I've been a little preoccupied. Is Hayley here?" I ask and that's when I hear her scream my name as she runs towards us.

Grabbing my hand she pulls me into her room to show me her new jewelry collection. I can't help but smile to watch the excitement in her face. Next, I learn about her new best friend at school and that she is starting a gymnastics class next month,

After dinner, Kristi and I sit outside on the patio, wrapped in blankets while Adam and Hayley play video games in the living room.

"The sky is so clear tonight, isn't it?" Kristi comments looking up.

"It is," I reply, leaning back in the chair and closing my eyes.

"Is everything okay Shelby?"

"Of course, why do you ask?" I reply, looking over at her.

"Shelby, I know you. You wear your emotions on your sleeve. What's going on?"

I take a deep breath. The last thing I want to do is discuss the actual things on my mind since I'm sure she will see me in a different light, I know she will. On the other hand if I were to ever tell a soul, she would be the one I would confide in.

"You have to promise me to keep this to yourself Kristi," I reply, looking directly into her eyes.

"You know I will Shelby, I always have."

"Okay," I exhale deeply. "I've been having an affair with a married man."

Kristi is silent, but looking at her she doesn't look shocked in the least bit.

"I knew it," she finally replies, taking me by surprise.

"What do you mean, you knew it?"

"I had a feeling. Call it a mother's intuition, even though I'm just your sister. Is it the man you mentioned a few months back? Your boss?"

"Yes."

"Oh boy Shelby," she says sinking into her chair. "I'm not going to lecture you or anything. You know it's wrong."

"I know," I say, hanging my head low and then I feel her hand on my arm.

"I'm not judging you and you're and adult so you make your own choices. I just don't want to see you hurt in the end. They never leave their wives," she says.

"I don't expect him to," I respond and she scrunches her forehead.

"So, this is just a sexual thing?" she questions.

"Yes. No. I don't know. It may have started out that way but I've fallen in love with him. He's amazing Kristi."

"But you don't expect him to leave his wife?"

"Okay, a part of me would really love him to leave her and be with me. The other part doesn't want to be the cause of breaking up a marriage."

"Well, with what the two of you are doing, you're not helping the marriage, that's for sure."

"I do realize that," I reply.

"Well, I'm glad that you felt that you could confide in me. I swear I will keep this to myself Shelby. I am here for you if you want to talk. In the end, you will do what is right for you," she pauses. "Can I ask you something?"

"Yes, of course," I say, wondering what she's about to ask.

"This trip to Las Vegas this weekend, was it with him?"

"Yes," I counter.

"I thought so," she smiles. "It's so unlike you to just spontaneously take a trip with a so-called friend. Did you have a good time?"

"It was amazing. Better than I could have ever imagined," I gush and she giggles.

Chapter Twenty

Vincent

Since returning from Vegas I've been finding it difficult to get away to spend time with Shelby. Monday's used to be a no brainer since Michelle would meet with her friends for the book club, but lately she hasn't been attending. She mentioned that she isn't interested in the book of choice and figures we could meet with friends for dinner instead. It's been a month and I've only been able to make it to Shelby's apartment three times, one of those times was just a very short visit where I took her in my arms and kissed her. I can see the disappointment in her eyes but she smiles and says she understands.

Thankfully, I can make tomorrow happen. Some of Michelle's friends have decided that they will be spending Saturday at the spa, dinner and a movie. It couldn't have come at a better time, I miss being with Shelby.

"Hey Vince," John says as he peeks into my office. "Shelby is having an issue with her printer. I've looked at it but couldn't figure it out. Want a shot at it?"

"Sure, let me see what I can do," I say getting up from my chair and making my way to Shelby's desk.

"Sorry Mr. Steele, I think I broke it," Shelby apologizes.

"I'm sure you didn't. Let's have a look. What's going on?"

"It just won't print. It worked fine this morning," she says and I take a look at a few different things.

After running the troubleshoot and fixing the error it's displaying on the screen, it still doesn't seem to work. I'm usually really good with these things but this one is throwing me for a loop. The printer is fairly old and has probably lived to its life expectancy.

"I think we may need to order a new one. It's just old and I think it gave up. Do you need to print something now?"

"I do actually," she smiles.

"You can come to my office to print. Just send it to my email," I offer and she leans, typing away on the keyboard. The sight alone is making my temperature rise.

Walking into my office I open my email to retrieve the document Shelby needs printed. Standing next to me, I lightly brush her hand with mine and she can't help but grin.

"I am really looking forward to tomorrow," I whisper. "God I miss you."

"I miss you too, you have no idea," she says. "Oh, did you want me to make lunch?"

"That sounds wonderful," I reply, removing the printed documents from the tray.

"Anything special or do you want to be surprised?"

"Surprised. You know I love surprises," I say and she gives me a naughty look.

"Well, I may have another in store for you tomorrow then," she winks before walking out of my office.

Adjusting my tie, I try to imagine what she could have in mind. Every minute spent with her is pure excitement and the moments escape too fast.

Wrapping up the day, I shut down my computer and gather my things. I was so immersed in my work that I didn't even notice it's already twenty minutes past the hour. As I pick up my blazer there is a slight knock on my door and I look up to find Shelby standing there focused in on me.

"Shelby," I say and she start starts walking towards me.

"Vincent," she counters, catching me off guard since she normally addresses me by my last name here in the office. "Don't worry. Everyone has already left."

Wrapping her arms around the back of my neck, she pulls me close, our lips barely touching. As she slowly licks my bottom lip I can feel myself become aroused and I go for a kiss. Next, her hands make their way to my belt, undoing the clasp and even though I should stop her, I can't. I suppose I'm already late, what's another half hour. Unbuttoning my pants and pulling down the zipper, she reaches in with her hand and the moment she touches me I let out a groan. Giving me one more kiss she sinks to her knees.

"Don't worry Vincent, I locked the front door."

Pulling up into the driveway my heart is still racing, how does she do this to me? Every single time. I'm pulled out of my thoughts by the sight of Luke's car and assume that he, Ashely and Libby will be joining us for dinner. Walking into the house, I am met by Michelle, Luke and Daniel, all wearing big smiles.

"Hey everyone," I begin. "Sorry I'm late. Where's everyone else?"

"Hey Dad, where's your cellphone?" Daniel asks and I pull it out of my pocket and within a second he takes it from me, setting it on the counter.

"What's going on?" I ask, wondering why he took my phone.

"Luke and Daniel decided that they are going to kidnap you for an ALL-GUYS weekend," Michelle beams and my expression is frozen.

"Oh guys, this weekend is real-"

"No dad, you're not getting out of this one. We already reserved a place at the Jersey Shore, we're going to have a great time," Luke grins.

"Oh another thing," Daniel starts. "No phones allowed."

"What are you talking about?" I reply.

"Well, the boys think if you take your phone you will spend the entire time working so they aren't taking theirs either."

"What if there is an emergency?" I ask.

"We will be fine, besides. Hotels have phones. Problem solved," Luke counters.

For a moment I try to think, I can't believe I have to cancel on Shelby, the both of us have been looking forward to tomorrow.

"Alight guys sounds great. I just need to message John inca-"

"Nope," Michelle laughs picking up my phone so I'm unable to grab it. "All taken care of. John knows you will be out of town. We were sneaky."

"Mom already packed your bag too. It's in the car," Daniel informs me and I hope my expression isn't representing how I am feeling right now.

"Okay. Let me just run up and get changed then and I'll be right down."

Standing in the bathroom I loosen my tie and pull it over my head. What am I going to do? How am I going to tell Shelby that I'm unable to make it? She will be expecting me tomorrow and I have no way of contacting her. This is the bad thing with cellphones, you don't remember anyone's phone number. I suppose I could call John and ask for Shelby's number but that would look very suspicious, especially since he knows I'm on a trip with my boys, why would I need her phone number? God damn it.

Luke is driving and I'm staring out of the passenger window. Then another thought hits me. Great, I'm sure Shelby will be sending me messages when I don't make it to her apartment and my phone is in Michelle's possession.

Thankfully I have a passcode and the messages don't reveal who it is until the phone is unlocked.

Shelby

I'm a little surprised to not hear from Vincent last night, he usually sends me a goodnight message. Well, I'm sure he must have fallen asleep early, it's happened before. I've already been to the grocery store and since Vincent will be here in a half hour, I start to cook. I decided on Beef Teriyaki with Rice and broccoli. I remember bringing this dish in for lunch once and he commented that it smelled amazing.

After setting the table I walk back into the kitchen and finish cooking. Checking the time on my phone I realize he must be running a little late so I set the burner on low and sit on the couch, catching up on the news. Glancing over at my phone again, I press the home button and the screen lights up. Fifteen minutes have passed, no message. It strikes me as a bit strange since he will usually send me a text, even if he's only going to be five minutes late. Picking up my phone I decide to send him a message to see if he's on his way, but he never replies. Walking into the kitchen I turn off the burners so the food doesn't dry out. After a half hour I send another message, asking if everything is okay, again, no response. Walking back into the kitchen, I place the food into storage containers and store them in the refrigerator. There's no way I can eat right now, I'm worried something must have happened to him. Even if it's not a good time, he makes sure to send me a sad face emoji, to tell me he can't talk. Two hours pass and still nothing. My thoughts are all over the place and I'm driving myself crazy. I need to get out of here for a bit so I decide to go on a run. I make sure to leave my phone at home because knowing myself, I would be checking it every two seconds and that would defeat the purpose of leaving in the fist place. Running helped for the moment, now that I'm done, my thoughts are running haywire again. I will just keep my fingers crossed that I have a message waiting for me when I get home. Before heading home, I stop at a smoothie place and while waiting in line I run into and old high school friend that I haven't seen in years. After ordering she asks if I have time to chat for a bit and a part of me wants to rush home but I decide to stay a bit longer. I wouldn't say we were close in school, more like acquaintances. I never let anyone get too close because of my family basically being nomads. Every time I found someone I really liked, we would move and I wasn't able to form real friendships until moving out of my parents home.

Returning home, I walk over to the counter and press the home button. No messages, no calls, nothing. What is going on?

Waking up the next day I check my phone again, nothing. Yesterday I was worried, today I am pissed off. I've had countless thoughts run through my head, one being, maybe he's through with me. Since getting back from Las Vegas I've barely seen him, what if that was his way of slowly distancing himself? Well, I think he would at least owe me a conversation. My emotions have definitely been on a rollercoaster and I decide to head to Kristi's house.

She is the only one that knows about Vincent and me and she's always had a way of bringing me back to my senses.

"Hey Shelby, I'm surprised to see you. You sounded a little upset on the phone," Kristi says as she answers the door.

"Yes. Can we talk somewhere privately?"

"Of course. Hayley is at the neighbor's house and Adam had to run to the mall. Do you want something to drink?" Kristi offers as I walk into the living room and take a seat on the couch.

"Just water. Thanks," I reply and she goes into the kitchen and returns with two glasses of water.

"Alright Shelby, what is it?"

"So Vincent was supposed to meet me for lunch yesterday. He never made it, no calls no messages. Then today comes around, still nothing," I explain.

"What are you thinking?"

"I don't know," I start. "First I thought something happened to him, then I thought he was done with me. For a moment I told myself that it may have slipped his mind but it doesn't explain the lack of communication."

"I see," she says, taking a sip of her water.

"What?"

"Well," she starts, setting her glass back on the coffee table. "Shelby, you have to realize something. He isn't yours. You have no claim to him whatsoever. I know it may not feel that way but the fact is, he is a married man. Who knows what happened, maybe there was a family emergency, maybe he lost his phone. Don't drive yourself crazy speculating. You've fallen too hard, like I said, you're going to end up with a broken heart."

"You're right. This isn't a regular relationship, even if he wanted to, he can't always be there," I say, feeling shattered.

"Hey," Kristi says grabbing my hand. "More than likely there will be a logical explanation for all this. If you want to continue being with him, then you are going to have to grow a thick skin and don't expect anything. I know, when you're with him I'm sure it feels like a full-blown relationship but that is not what the two of you have, you are the other woman. His family comes first. What are you thinking right now?"

"I was just thinking that if something ever happened to him I wouldn't know until I came into work. If he were in the hospital I wouldn't even be able to call since I'm not next of kin."

"That's very true."

Back at home, I realize the talk with my sister definitely opened my eyes to a few things and I feel calm. I've never been in a situation like this and she's correct, I have no rights to him, I'm just the other woman. Looking back at this weekend I almost don't recognize the person I was, I know it was mainly driven by fear, fear that Vincent had gotten hurt or that he changed his mind. I can't let fear take over, I need to take a deep breath, hold my head up and keep going.

Chapter Twenty-One

Vincent

I must admit, this guy's weekend was a fantastic idea and I'm so thankful that the boys set this up. We spent most of Saturday at Casino Pier, rode a few rides, walked on the beach and went Go Kart Racing. After dinner we stopped by a store, picked up a few beers, played cards and shared some great laughs. We really should do this more often, even if it's just a ballgame or dinner. Even though we had a wonderful time, my thoughts would drift to Shelby at times, wishing I could have at least sent her a quick message. She must be wondering what the hell happened to me.

We just made it back home and I'm opening the trunk to get my suitcase. Luke says he's going to head home to Ashely and Libby.

"Hey Dad, I think I'm going to crash here. I don't have to work until noon tomorrow anyway," Daniel says, grabbing his suitcase out of the trunk as well.

"I drove you here, how are you going to get home?" Luke asks.

"Mom or I will just drive him on our way to work," I say and Luke starts to chuckle.

"Well, good luck getting him moving so early in the morning."

"Well, we have many years of practice," I laugh and Michelle comes outside to greet us.

"Did you guys have a good time?" she asks. "Do you boys want to stay for dinner?"

"Luke said he's heading home but Daniel is staying the night," I explain and after saying our goodbyes to Luke, we walk into the house.

Taking my suitcase upstairs, I unpack and I feel Michelle standing behind me. Turning around I see her standing there with my phone in her hand. For a second, I'm a bit worried. I know there's no way she could have seen if anyone texted, but if Shelby happened to call, that definitely would have shown up on the screen. I didn't even think of that.

"Hey," I say as she hands me the phone.

"This thing was going off non-stop the other day. You really need to unsubscribe from some websites, they will clog up your inbox," she says and I'm relieved.

"I know," I begin. "You're right. I always complain about that."

As Michelle leaves the room, I put in my passcode and see I have four messages from Shelby, less than I initially thought. After reading the messages I can tell she was worried and I assumed as much. I start typing a message *Shelby, I am sorry, something came up and had to go out of town. We will talk tomorrow!*

Putting my toiletries in the bathroom I walk back into the bedroom and my phone chimes. Unlocking the screen, I swipe the notification and it's from Shelby saying *I'm glad you're okay, talk to you tomorrow xoxo.*

At dinner, Michelle shares that she and her friends had a great day at the spa and dinner but skipped the movie, returning to our house instead. Our conversation shifts to all of the things we did while away and Michelle was surprised to hear that I had a few beers. If I drink alcohol it's usually wine, beer has never been one of my go to beverages.

I have a hard time finding sleep that night, and I'm not sure why. I should be tired, but keep tossing and turning. Picking up the phone from my nightstand, I scroll through my email inbox. Moments later I find myself drifting, the phone falling out of my hands. Looking through boring emails will definitely do that.

Shelby

I am running so late this morning. I thought I only hit snooze once but apparently, I must have turned the alarm off all together. If I'm lucky, I will make it into work right on time. Rushing out the door and to my car, my heel gets stuck on a broken piece of cement on the sidewalk and of course, it snaps off. This really isn't my morning. Stumbling back up the stairs, I walk back into my apartment and throw on a new pair. Thankfully I own several pairs of black pumps.

Before I start driving, I send Vincent a text, letting him know I may be a few minutes late. Tossing my phone on the passenger's seat, I start the car and hurry to the office. Once I arrive, I grab my phone and purse from the seat and rush inside.

"Morning Shelby," John says holding a cup of coffee in his hand, I'm sure Vincent made it this morning.

"Good morning, sorry I'm late," I say, setting my purse on the desk and reaching to turn on my computer.

"Oh, no problem. Technically you're right on time," he chuckles.

Immediately the phone starts to ring and since it's a Monday, I know I probably won't have a free moment until lunch. I have yet to see Vincent, I've barely had time to step away from my desk. Finishing setting up an

197

appointment on the phone, Vincent steps out of his office with a client and they both walk towards me.

"Shelby, could you check my schedule and see if I have any openings next Wednesday afternoon?"

"Yes sir," I reply, pulling up his schedule. "You have a 4 pm appointment left."

"Mrs. Figueroa, will that time work for you?" Vincent asks and she agrees. "Wonderful, it was a pleasure to meet you and again, if you have any questions in the meantime, just give me a call."

Vincent returns to his office and I put the appointment into the system, handing Mrs. Figueroa a card with the date and time. Once she leaves, my phone chimes and I pick it up and see the message is from Vincent asking me to come into his office. Standing in the doorway I knock on the open door and he looks up, smiling as soon as he sees me.

"Shelby, can you shut the door behind you?" he asks and I do so.

He gets up from his desk and walks towards me, taking me in his arms and squeezing me tight. Wrapping my arms around him, I close my eyes and rest my head on his shoulder. He kisses the top of my head before moving back and looking into my eyes.

"I am so sorry about this weekend," he begins. "When I got home on Friday my sons basically kidnapped me and took me to the Jersey Shore for the three of us to spend some time together."

"Well, that was a nice surprise," I smile, relieved it wasn't anything terrible.

"It was. I would have messaged you to let you know but as soon as I walked in the house, Daniel grabbed my phone, saying no electronics allowed."

"Oh my god," I say, covering my mouth. "Did your wife see my messages?"

"No, she didn't. I use a passcode and my messages don't show a preview on the screen."

"I was so worried that something happened to you," I say pulling him close.

"I figured you would be and I really wish I could have let you know."

"I understand Vincent, these things will happen from time to time. That's life," I reply and he kisses me, god have I missed those lips.

Suddenly there is a knock at the door and we immediately jump back and I grab a file off his desk, taking a seat in the chair. Returning to his chair, Vincent says to come in and the door opens and John is standing there.

"Am I interrupting something?" John asks with questioning eyes.

"Not at all," Vincent replies and John steps in, closing the door behind him.

Once the two of them are lost in conversation about an upcoming case, I figure it's the perfect time to excuse myself and go back to my desk.

As the day comes to a close I shut down my computer and switch the phone over to the answering machine. As I put on my coat, Vincent walks out of his office, giving me a smile.

"Have a good night Shelby," he says, and a part of me is a little saddened that I won't see him after work today.

"Thank you, Mr. Steele," I answer. "I hope you have a great night as well."

Instead of going straight home, I stop at the grocery store on the way to pick up a few things. Standing in front of the yogurt aisle I ponder what to get as a familiar voice says my name.

"Shelby?"

"Chad?" I reply when I see my Ex standing there with a big smile.

"How are you? You look great," he says, leaning in and giving me an unexpected and awkward hug.

"I'm doing great, how are you?"

"I'm good. Lots of changes in my life," he begins. "I'm engaged and I'm going to be a dad."

"What?" I reply, as if I didn't hear him.

"Yeah, isn't that crazy? I never thought my life would take that direction," he smiles.

"That's great Chad, I am really happy for you," I say and he continues talking, telling me about his fiancé, his new job and him quitting alcohol all together. There is this minuscule part of me that does feel a bit of sadness because he never felt the need to be proactive and change his life while he was with me. In any case, I truly am happy for him and his fiancé and wish them the best for the future. After completing my shopping, I drive home and park in my usual spot. Taking the bags out of the trunk of my car I head inside my apartment building and walk up the stairs. When I get to my floor I look up and freeze.

"Vincent?" I say, a little shocked.

"Hello darling," he replies coming to grab the bags from me.

"Oh my god, how long have you been waiting here?"

"I just got here about two minutes ago."

"Wait," I start. "Did you tell me you were coming over and I totally blanked?"

"No, it was a surprise," he says as I unlock the door. "I missed you."

As we walk inside Vincent sets my grocery bags on the kitchen counter and he begins to unpack them, placing the milk and cheese into the refrigerator. As I'm about to put the bag of rice into the pantry, I feel Vincent's right arm wrap around my waist and he moves my hair to the left side, exposing my neck and kissing it. We spend the next twenty minutes talking, kissing, just enjoying every minute we have together. This is what I love about us, it's not just about sex. Sure, sex was the foundation and back then I never would have expected to feel this bond, this connection, but it's there.

Chapter Twenty-Two

Shelby

Since I will be in Boston for Hayley's actual birthday next weekend, I decide to take her out for an all-day shopping trip in the city. I'm really glad Kristi decided to join us even though she's never been much of a shopper. To kick off the day, we stop at a nail salon to get pedicures. Hayley insists that the three of us use the same color and after browsing all of the choices, she comes running up with a bottle of hot pink nail polish. I should have known, if you give her a choice, it will always be pink. Luckily the salon isn't very busy and we all get a seat next to one another. It's adorable to watch Hayley's eyes focus on the nail designer as she begins to paint her nails, the smile on her face is priceless.

Our next stop is a popular jewelry store in the mall, costume jewelry of course. As Hayley browses the aisles with her basket, Kristi and I try on ridiculous looking sunglasses and almost die from laughter. A few minutes later Hayley comes up to us and I'm completely surprised that she doesn't have one item in her basket.

"Is there nothing you liked?" I ask, putting away the glasses with attached bunny ears.

"Well, there is something I want," she begins and looks over at her mom. "I want my ears pierced."

"Hayley," Kristi begins. "Are you sure that is what you want?"

For a moment I can see Hayley debating. There was a time last year that Hayley said she wanted to get her ears pierced. Kristi told me she was sitting in the chair and right before the attendant could press the lever, Hayley screamed for them to stop.

"I really want earrings," Hayley says. "I'm a little scared though."

"Hayley," I start. "Do you want to watch me go first?"

"Did your holes close up?" Kristi asks, looking at my earlobe.

"No, I can just get my cartilage pierced though," I reply and Hayley smiles, looking a bit more relieved.

After choosing a small white stone, I sit in the chair and the employee marks the top of my right ear. After lining the gun up with the mark she made, I hear a loud click and my ear immediately begins to burn. I make sure to keep a smile on my face, the earlobes won't be half as bad.

As Hayley bravely sits in the chair, she grabs each one of our hands and closes her eyes tightly. About ten seconds later, the right earlobe is done and she opens her eyes, wearing a big smile. After finishing the left side the employee hands Hayley a mirror so she can see her new earrings.

"I love it," she beams. "It didn't even hurt that bad."

After paying we make our way to the food court and decide to have lunch before continuing with the rest of the mall. Sitting at a table near the entrance, the three of us are in the middle of a conversation as we are interrupted by an unfamiliar voice saying my name. Looking up I'm staring right at Mrs. Steele, oh my god.

"Mrs. Steele," I say, not exactly sure what else to say at this point.

"I told Vince it was you," she smiles and that's when Vincent walks up.

"Hello Shelby," he says, keeping a business-like expression.

"Mr. Steele," I reply. "Oh I'm sorry, this is my sister Kristi and my niece Hayley."

"It's a pleasure to meet you," Vincent says as he shakes Kristi's hand. "I'm Vincent Steele and this is my wife Michelle."

These had to have been the most awkward five minutes I've experienced in a long time. Well, the Christmas Party wasn't a walk in the park either. I think what made me feel a bit more uncomfortable was that I told Kristi about Vincent and I. Hiding those thoughts in the back of my mind, Kristi, Hayley and I finish out lunch and continue our day of shopping.

Once we get back to Kristi's house, she offers to make up some coffee and Hayley goes to a neighbor's house to play. Sitting on the couch, Kristi walk into the living room, handing me a cup.

"You can say it." I begin. "I know you want to."

"Well," she begins. "That definitely was awkward."

"I agree," I reply, taking a sip of my coffee.

"I can see what drew you to him, he is very charismatic, charming...and I will say he is a very good-looking man as well."

"I know," I swoon.

"How do you feel about the run in?"

"With his wife?" I ask.

"Yes."

"Well, I met her at the Christmas Party," I say.

"Oh, that's right," she leans back, drinking her coffee. "Do you ever feel guilty Shelby?"

"All the time. Well, most of the time," I begin. "When I see her, it's makes it real. To tell the truth when it's me and him, I sometimes forget that he is married. I know it probably sounds stupid."

"It doesn't," Kristi counters. "You've fallen in love with him. I can't understand that."

"I have," I sigh.

I end up staying the night at my sister's house. Why go back to an empty apartment with no one waiting for me? That is the downside to my relationship. He will never be there waiting for me to get home, with the exception of the other day. A smile comes over my face when I think of him

206

standing in front of my door, totally unexpected. Maybe he and I will be together one day.

It's finally Thursday and I thought this day would never come. I know it feels like it's gone by so slow because of my anticipation for our trip to Boston. Vincent had planned to come over after work yesterday but unfortunately had to cancel. Even though I understand and would never hold it against him, it still hurts me deep down inside. Oh well, head up and move on, at least I will have him this weekend.

"Hello," I hear a voice pull me out of my daydream.

"I'm so sorry," I say, looking up and seeing a man standing in front of me with the most magical green eyes I've ever seen. "How can I help you?"

"I have an appointment at 3 pm with Mr. Baker I believe," this stranger responds with a smile. "My name is Javier Cruz."

After checking him in I ask him to have a seat and he smiles before walking toward the row of chairs against the wall. As I continue working, I can't help but steal a glance every so often. He is definitely gorgeous, everything from his hair to the way he dresses. Suddenly our eyes connect again and I scold myself for being so obvious. Smiling I return my eyes to the screen and type absolutely nothing, feeling like an idiot.

"Excuse me," he says as he gets up from his chair coming my way.

"Yes sir?" I reply.

"May I ask your name?" he smiles.

"My name?" I ask, slapping myself mentally. "It's Shelby Hunter."

"Shelby. May I call you Shelby?"

"Sure," I respond.

"Shelby, I just wanted to say you have a very beautiful smile."

"Wow. Thank you so much," I say, totally aware that I am blushing.

"Mr. Cruz?" John calls as he walks up to my desk.

Perfect timing. I have no idea what I would have said next. Okay Shelby, some guy gave you a compliment, it's not the first this has happened. There was something about him, I can't pinpoint it though. Something that made my heart beat a bit faster. For a moment I feel guilty. My heart belongs to Vincent, why would I even look at another man in this way? I have the man that makes me feel like I am the most important thing in the world. Well, actually I don't have him and I don't know if I ever will.

Forty-five minutes later John comes up to my desk with Mr. Cruz and asks me to schedule another appointment.

"Alright," I say looking through the schedule on the computer. "How about March 23rd at 3 pm again?"

"That's perfect," he responds and I write the date on Johns business card, before handing it over.

"Listen, I don't want to come off as too forward but I was wondering if you happened to be single?" he asks, taking me by surprise.

"Umm," I start before my thoughts are interrupted by Vincent walking by, heading toward John's office. "I'm not. I'm sorry."

"Well, it was worth a shot," he smiles, looking a bit disappointed. "I will see you in two weeks. Have a great day."

As soon as he is gone I lean back in my chair, running my hands through my hair. For a moment, I thought about going for it, technically I am single. Seeing Vincent walk by, smiling in my direction made me feel like a terrible person for even having that thought.

Before leaving work, Vincent brushes my hand ever so slightly and I look up to see his eyes smiling at me. Yes, I did the right thing.

Chapter Twenty-Three

Vincent

Boston! We've finally arrived. Walking into the lobby of the hotel we see quite a long line at the reception desk. As soon as we stand in line, a woman in front of us turns around and starts to talk. She looks to be in her early twenties with three little children, one an infant that she is holding.

"I've been standing in line forever. I think they may be training someone up there. Normally I wouldn't care but with my husband not being here…well, it's been a stressful day."

"It definitely looks as if you have your hands full," Shelby says. "How old is the little one?"

"He is six months old, I swear, this is my last," the woman chuckles.

Shelby and the woman continue to talk as I scroll through my phone, checking my emails. Suddenly one of her other kids tugs at her purse and all of it's contents fall to the ground. Kneeling down I pick up the items and place them back into her purse.

"Oh thank you so much," she smiles and at that moment, the baby starts screaming.

She looks beyond stressed and at this point I would love to take her to the front of the line so she can get checked into her room. As she tries to soothe the infant, her daughter asks to be picked up.

"Honey, I can't pick you up, I'm sorry," she pleads.

"If you want I can hold your baby, maybe I can get him to stop crying," Shelby offers and I have never seen anyone hand a child off so fast.

As soon as the boy is in Shelby's arms, he calms down a bit and for a moment I take in that image. She looks so happy talking to the little guy, even her eyes are sparkling. I know that she would make a wonderful mother. The way she talks about her niece, the excitement in her voice. Then a thought hits me. Say she and I continue this relationship, it would rob her of the opportunity to have a family of her own. Even if for some reason, she and I happened to end up together somehow, I don't want any more children. My time has come and gone and I have two great boys.

As we continue to stand in line, Shelby holds the baby for the woman, making life a bit easier on her. Once she's checked in, the woman grabs the boy and thanks us for our help. After we check in, we head toward the elevator in order to get to our floor. This time I wasn't able to book adjoining rooms but since the seminar isn't being held in this hotel, I'm not too worried about it. Actually, the seminar is about ten miles away from here and I doubt anyone I know will be staying here.

Reaching the room, we get settled and Shelby lies down on the bed, signaling for me to join her. Lying on top of her, her hand envelopes the back of my neck, pulling me towards her lips and kissing me sensually before pausing to look at me.

"I've really been looking forward to this," she smiles. "Just having you to myself again for a bit. Being able to fall asleep and wake up next to you. I think that's one of the things I miss the most."

"Me too," I counter, kissing her neck.

"Well," she chuckles. "I must admit, I really missed this as well."

Continuing with my mouth on her neck, I being undoing the buttons of her blouse before traveling down to her jeans. It's not often that I see her dressed casually and I love it. It doesn't take long for me to remove every single piece of her clothing, tossing them on the floor. Undoing my pants, her hand slips underneath the waistband of my boxers, grasping me and slowly moving up and down. I know I will never tire of her, how could I?

Shelby

Every moment with him is one I keep locked away in my heart. This man is everything I've ever wanted, ever dreamed of. With my head on his chest, he lightly runs his fingertips over my lower back.

"Shelby, do you want to have children?" Vincent asks, surprising me a little.

"Umm," I reply, pausing for a long time. "I can't."

"What do you mean?" he counters, a little perplexed.

"It's a long story."

"You know I love listening to your stories," he replies.

"Ok," I say pausing. "When I was twenty-two I met my boyfriend Jason while I was working at a restaurant part-time. He asked me out on a date and soon after we fell in love. After about six months of dating I got pregnant and after we both recovered from the unexpected news, we started to plan our life together. Even though we didn't know each other very long, our families were very supportive. We moved in together and things were going great. I had no issues during the pregnancy, no morning sickness, no heartburn. I still remember sitting on the couch one night, feeling the first kick, it's a moment I will never forget. At the anatomy scan we found out we were having a boy and I remember myself crying for joy. The next few months were spent preparing for our little boy's arrival. We didn't have much money, but our families helped out a lot. When I was seven months pregnant we went to my monthly prenatal appointment and the doctor couldn't find the heartbeat. After performing an ultrasound, they told us our son had passed away. I couldn't believe what I heard, I swore I felt him kicking before the appointment. Because I was so far along, my doctor told me he would need to induce labor and I would have to deliver my son.

I don't remember much of the labor, I blocked it out. Once he was born, they showed him to me and I remember losing it. It's one of the worst things I've ever had to go through in my entire life. As the doctor was delivering the afterbirth they noticed an abnormal amount of bleeding that they weren't able to control, that's when I passed out. When I woke up I was told they had to perform a hysterectomy to save my life. So long story short, I'm missing the parts needed to have children."

He immediately grabs me and holds me tight and that is exactly what I needed. No one besides my family knows about my son, I never felt the need to share him with anyone that has come into my life.

"I am so sorry Shelby, I can't even imagine that feeling. How did you work through it? Was your boyfriend supportive?"

"He left me about two months later. He had a very hard time with everything that happened and ended up moving out. He met someone else fairly soon and they ended up having a family together."

"Oh my god, that is terrible. Oh Shelby," Vincent replies, full of concern.

"You know, you are the first guy I've ever shared that with," I say and he looks at me a bit surprised. "Well, I've always disclosed that I am unable to have kids to anyone I've dated but never have told them the full extent as to why not. I've never felt this close to someone before, never this connected."

"I feel the same way Shelby," he says. "I can't imagine how hard it's been on you."

"It definitely makes dating very difficult. Once I would share my inability to conceive, they usually ended up leaving me soon after, saying it had nothing to do with me. I knew better, but there was nothing I could do. I felt so inadequate. Then came Chad. He made it very clear that he never wanted kids and I really thought I found my perfect match. Obviously, he wasn't, but I believe I stayed with him for so long because he accepted me along with my flaw."

"Shelby, you are not flawed. Don't ever think that," Vincent says, grabbing my hand and holding it. "You are so young and I feel I haven't experienced half of what you have."

"That's a blessing, believe me."

"Can I ask you something very personal? If you'd rather not answer I completely understand," Vincent asks and I nod.

"Where did you lay your son to rest?"

"A cemetery about an hour south of where I live now. My parents still live in the town. I visit him often. Even after all these years, I miss him. I'm probably crazy, my son never even took a breath but I feel like I lost a piece of me after losing him."

"You are not crazy. It is completely normal. You carried him for seven months, you formed a bond."

"Yeah," I say, feeling my eyes water a bit.

"Come here," Vincent says, pulling me close to him and I immediately start to cry. I usually do my best not to show any signs of weakness but with him I feel as if I can let go. We spend the next ten minutes in each other's arms and he runs his fingers through my hair, kissing my forehead.

Chapter Twenty-Four

Vincent

There was no way I could have just gotten up and left her, even if she hadn't been crying. The fact that she felt comfortable enough to share that part of her life with me left me honored. To be honest, it's crossed my mind many times, wondering if I am wasting her time when she could be meeting someone and starting a family. Knowing that it is impossible really makes me wonder if she and I were meant to be. At my age I obviously have no interest in having more children. In that regard, she and I would definitely be a match. I know she has fallen in love with me and even though I've fought with myself, today I realized that I am in love with her. As she lies in my arms I move my lips close to her ear and whisper Ya tebe kahayu.

She looks up at me with a smile, asking what I just said. I stare into those beautiful green eyes and take a deep breath.

"I love you," I reply and she covers her mouth. "I mean it. I love you Shelby. I believe I've loved you from the start, it just took me this long to admit it to myself."

"I love you too, Vincent," she says, placing her hand on my neck, kissing me slowly.

We spent the rest of the day in the room, wrapped in each other's arms, taking advantage of not having any restriction on time or obligations. Tonight, it's just us and I wish it could always be this way.

I feel as if I blinked and our weekend has already come to and end. When we were in Las Vegas we had an amazing time but Boston brought us closer together, connected us in a way I never expected. Her opening herself up to me, trusting me with her pain is something I hold dear to my heart.

As I pull up to the house I see Michelle coming outside, walking to the mailbox. Getting out of the car I pop the trunk, grabbing my suitcase.

"Hi Honey," she says, walking up to me, kissing me. "How was the seminar?"

"It was okay," I reply. "Mail on Sunday?"

"No," she laughs. "I was lazy and didn't check it yesterday. Perfect timing, I'm about to cook. The boys are coming over."

"Both of them?"

"Yes, they were going to come by yesterday but decided that they would wait until you are back home. Speaking of the boys, looks like Daniel is pulling up."

Once everyone arrives and Michelle finishes cooking we sit at the table to enjoy dinner. Even though I am physically sitting here, in my mind I am very far away. On my flight home, a very serious thought ran through my head. I thought about leaving Michelle and starting a life with Shelby. I would say I felt quite confident in my proposed decision but sitting here at dinner with my family, my wife who's been by my side for twenty-six years, things are becoming very cloudy. Yes, I am definitely unhappy in my marriage, have been for a long time. The lack of connection, the non-existent intimacy, the arguments. Those are clear signs but throwing away twenty-six years and the life we've built for another woman seems like the most irresponsible decision I could make. I'm well aware that I can't continue living this double life forever and will have to make a decision one day but today is not that day.

Once everyone leaves, Michelle and I head upstairs to go to bed. It's still early but I'm exhausted, physically and mentally. After brushing my teeth, I get into bed and Michelle turns around, wrapping her arm around me.

"I missed you Vince," she says, kissing me.

"I missed you to," I reply and she pulls me closer to her, closing her eyes and resting her head on my shoulder. Kissing her forehead, I turn off the lamp on my nightstand and go to sleep.

I spend most of my day at court the next day but still manage to have a few minutes with Shelby once I return to the office.

"How was court?" she asks, our arms still wrapped around one another.

"Excellent, no loss today," I reply.

"Wow, maybe this will be your new lucky tie," she grins.

"Maybe," I start. "Do you like this one?"

"Well, it does have something. The pattern is interesting. I never would have thought to put stripes and a damask pattern together."

"My son got it for me for Christmas and I figured it was time to wear it," I say and she places her hands on my face, pulling me down toward her lips.

Shelby

A month has gone by and I'm seeing less and less of Vincent. It seems as if something keeps coming between us. If it's not one thing it's another. The other day he finally made it to my place and we immediately began tearing each other's clothes off. About two minutes later he got a phone call from his son saying his car broke down on the way to work, and he was stuck on the highway. Of course he had to go, family is always first, as it should be. I find myself wondering more lately, wondering how long we can keep this up, wondering if this may be the beginning of our flame going out. I'm the one sitting here by myself, I have plenty of time to think and to tell the truth, I am lonely every night. I know he could never just come spend the night here with me and I always have to rely on seminars for a weekend getaway. Speaking of seminars, there is another one coming up two weeks from now in New Orleans and I can't wait to accompany him there. If I had a bucket list, that city would definitely be on it.

Walking into Vincent's office with a stack of files, I close the door behind me before walking toward his desk. Smiling at me he gets up and meets me halfway, taking the files out of my hands, and tossing them in a chair. Turning me and setting me on his desk he spreads my legs and moves closer, moving my hair to the side and kissing my neck. I know this is about how far it will go since the others are in the building, but this will keep me going for a few days.

"So," he says between kisses. "I reserved a hotel in the French quarter. I think you're going to love it."

"I honestly don't care where we are, as long as I'm with you," I reply.

"You are so wonderful Shelby. I can't wait to get away with you. I feel terrible for canceling on you so much."

"It's not your fault, it's just been a difficult month."

"Tell me about it," he pauses. "I still have to book our flights. I meant to do that the other day but never got around to it."

"Well, I'm excited," I smile. "I've always wanted to see New Orleans."

"I will be glad to take you. Do you have plans on Thursday?"

"Thursday? No, why?" I reply and he grins from ear to ear. "Oh wow, I don't think you've ever come by on a Thursday."

"Well, if it were up to me I would be there every day of the week," he says kissing me one more time.

Back at my desk it amazes me how one little smile of his can drown all of my sorrows. No one has ever been able to do that, I've never let anyone this close. A few minutes later, the phone rips me from my thoughts and I get back to work.

Days seem like years when you're waiting for something, but we've finally made it to Thursday. I just got to my apartment and Vincent should be here any second. Walking into my bedroom I decide to change clothes before he gets here. As soon as I unbutton my blouse, there is a knock at the door. Holding it together I walk into the living room to answer the door.

"Getting started without me?" Vincent asks as he comes in, closing the door behind him.

"Maybe," I reply, biting my lip.

Moments later, he has me on the couch, with my skirt up to my hips, removing my panties and throwing them across the room. My body craves him and I can see the longing in his eyes. Within seconds we are lost in one another and it brings back memories from our first encounter. Collapsed on top of me, Vincent's hand is in mine, holding it tightly and I could fall asleep with him right here. Kissing my shoulder, he starts to get up, surprising me just a little.

"What's the matter?" I ask.

"I can't stay. Michelle has invited some friends over for a late dinner tonight and I have to stop by the store to pick up more wine."

"Oh," I say, sitting up and pulling my skirt back down. "Was the dinner planned?"

"Yes," he replies. "Why?"

"Just curious. Doesn't she have a community meeting on Thursday's?"

"Normally she does but it was cancelled. Okay darling, I have to run," he says, bending down and kissing my lips. "Love you."

"I love you too," I reply and with that he is out of the door.

Sitting on the couch a number of things run through my head. I can't pinpoint it but for some reason I feel a bit used. He came here, knowing he couldn't stay, yet failed to mention it to me before. He came here, had his fun and now he's off to a dinner party that Michelle has planned. Don't get me wrong, I had my fun as well but now I'm left with this empty feeling in the pit of my stomach. Then my thoughts turn to the last thing he said before walking out the door. He said he loved me. I hadn't heard that since Boston and I figured it may have been a fluke in a way. Now I feel ridiculous for thinking negatively of him, I knew this would be hard, but I couldn't have known how hard.

Chapter Twenty-Five

Vincent

It was great having our friends over tonight. Such a wonderful evening with lots of laughs and old stories. Once everyone leaves, I help Michelle with the dishes in the kitchen. While wiping the countertops Michelle makes a suggestion that stops me in my tracks.

"What did you say?" I ask as if I didn't hear her.

"I said I'd like to go to New Orleans with you," she smiles and, in my mind, I'm thinking of things to say that will make her reconsider.

"Honey, it's a seminar. You know I'm going to be very busy."

"That's alright, I'm sure they won't keep you all hours of the night," she grins, washing her hands.

"What are you going to do all day?"

"Well I can do a little shopping. Explore the area, you know, tourist things," she replies and I can feel a bead of sweat building near my eyebrow.

"Explore the area? We've been to New Orleans many times, what's left to explore?" I counter.

"Vince, do you not want me to come?" she asks, looking directly at me.

"Of course, I want you to come," I say, feeling defeated. "I just wanted to make sure you wouldn't be bored sitting around."

That night as I lie in bed, I stare up at the ceiling, wondering how the hell I am going to break this to Shelby. We have been looking forward to this trip for some much needed time alone. Just in the last month I've had to give her several rainchecks, and I feel terrible. There was something about the look in her eye today that caught my attention, a sadness I haven't seen before. I wish I could have stayed, asked what was going on. What happened to the times where we saw each other several times a week?

Grabbing the phone off my nightstand I decide to message Shelby, telling her goodnight and that I love her. Within minutes my phone buzzes and after opening the message screen it's a return message from Shelby reading *I love you too Vincent.* Reading her words brings a smile to my lips and I close my eyes and go to sleep.

The next day at the office I know I should tell Shelby about the trip but I can't get myself to do it. Walking out of my office I stand there for a moment, taking her in. She's sitting at her desk talking to Bryce. A moment later, both start to laugh and I smile. Hearing her laugh is one of the most beautiful sounds in the world. There's no way I can cast a storm over her right now.

"Oh, hey Vince," Bryce starts. "Sorry did you need Shelby?"

"Yes," I begin, knowing I have to do this. "When you get a moment could you stop by my office, it's regarding your leave."

"Of course, Mr. Steele," she says, getting up and following me into my office.

After closing the door, all I want to do is grab her, hold her tight and kiss her until it hurts, but that is not the reason I asked her to come in. Taking a deep breath, I close my eyes and exhale. I feel Shelby's hand on mine, gently moving her thumb over my knuckles.

"What's the matter?" she asks, sounding concerned.

"Shelby," I say looking into those beautiful green eyes full of love. "I can't take you to New Orleans."

"What do you mean? We jus-"

"Michelle said she's going," I say interrupting her.

"Oh," she says, removing her hand from mine and adjusting her collar just a bit.

"She told me yesterday at dinner. I am so sorry Shelby, I feel horrible."

"It's not your fault," she replies and I can tell she's hurt, very hurt. "I understand. Will I see you before you leave?"

"You will," I assure her. "I will make it happen. One way or another."

She steps towards me, pulling me in, her head resting on my chest. My fingers brush through her hair and I kiss the top of her head. At the same time, I am trying to think of

227

when I will be able to get away from home for a bit, and not just for fifteen minutes. I know she deserves more than that, more than I can give her, but the thought of ever letting her go feels like a knife stabbing right into my heart.

It's Saturday and the kids are over for dinner tonight. Libby, Jackson and I are in the living room, building towers out of wooden blocks. Well, Libby and I are, Jackson's idea of fun is running into them, making Libby very angry.

"Alright everyone," Michelle announces. "Dinner is done, let's eat."

Sitting down at the table, Michelle has prepared chicken pot pie, one of Ashely's favorites. Even after asking Michelle for the recipe and making it herself, she still prefers Michelle's. I will admit, it's very delicious. While eating, Ashley and Michelle's conversations grabs my attention and I listen closely.

"So when is it Ashely?" Michelle asks.

"Next Saturday. I'd love for you to come. My mom and sister will be there as well."

"What is it?" I ask, nonchalant.

"Oh it's a festival about forty-five minutes north of here. It's called Ladies Day and it's a huge fair with everything from craft, food, live music and much more."

"I don't know. Maybe Vince an-"

"You should go," I blurt out, almost too quickly. "I think you will have a wonderful time."

For a moment Michelle gives me a look as if I've backed her into a corner and to be honest I did. It's probably terrible that I have my own agenda, but I saw the chance and took it. After a little hesitation she agrees and the conversation turns to Jackson new daycare.

Shelby

I just got a text from Vincent saying he will be available next Saturday and would love to spend the day with me. I'm honestly kind of surprised to read the words *spend the day* since anything over thirty minutes is rare nowadays. Of course, this week feels like it's dragging on, we've stayed fairly busy but I think the anticipation of Saturday is getting to me. John just came up to my desk and asked if I would pick up some assorted pastries from the bakery a few blocks away. He and Vincent have a meeting with two lawyers from another firm in about an hour here at our office.

"I'd do it but my appointment will probably be here any minute. Can you get four ice coffee's as well?"

"Of course Mr. Baker," I reply as Vincent comes walking up to us.

"John, how is she going to carry all of that?" Vincent asks, shaking his head. "Here, I'll go with you. I'm free until the meeting anyway."

"Thank you, Mr. Steele," I reply, grabbing my purse from the floor.

"Vince, do you need cash?" John asks and he shakes his head no.

As I get into Vincent's car, I reminisce about the first time I sat in this very seat. After putting on my seatbelt Vincent starts the car, but before shifting, he grabs my hand, kissing it softly. The drive doesn't take long but I cherish every single moment I get to have with him.

Once we get to the bakery, we place our order and wait, looking at all of the photographs on the wall. The bakery is called 53 and every fifty-third customer of the day has their photo taken and it's put up on this very wall. As the barista serves the person that came in after us, we find out she is number fifty-three. Come to find out, she gets a free coffee as well. Turning to Vincent, I smile and he opens his mouth as if he wants to say something.

"Yes?" I ask.

"We could have been fifty-three," he responds.

"You're right. Lucky we weren't."

"Would it be so bad?" he asks and I raise my eyebrow.

"Well, then we would have our photograph on this wall," I counter and he grins.

"Colleagues getting coffee together, nothing wrong with that."

"Well, more like boss and employee," I smile and before he can say anything else, Vincent's name is called, letting us know our order is ready.

It's finally Saturday and I'm waiting for Vincent to show up. A part of me is waiting for that phone call that yet another thing came up and he won't be able to make it. About ten minutes later the door bell rings and I sigh in relief. Running to the door I open it and there he is, eyes beaming at me. Immediately I fall into his arms, at this point I don't care that we haven't even made it in the door, neither does he. Once we finally make it inside, passion completely takes over and we find ourselves in my bed. Caressing my body with his lips he takes his time and I am savoring every minute. There's no rush, no haste, just slow sensual declarations of love that I have longed for. An hour later we finally collapse, recovering from one of the most beautiful experiences of my life. Actually, to be honest, it would be hard to choose one, Vincent has given me so many. Holding me in his arms, I can feel his heart beating. My fingers gently run up and down his arm until his hand finds mine, spreading my fingers with his.

"I've missed being this close to you," he says and I move my head up, kissing his jawline.

"Me too," I reply.

We spend the next two hours together, talking, laughing and enjoying each other's company. It's in these moments I forget all of my fears and concerns about what we are. Right now, we are Shelby and Vincent, two people who love each other and that is all that matters.

"Shit," Vincent says, looking at his phone. "I have to go."

"I wish you could stay," I reply and he pulls me close and holds me tight.

"I think I would never leave again," he whispers, and I smile.

Walking him to the door, he kisses me one more time before twisting the handle. Telling him goodbye, he walks out but stops after about five steps and turns around.

Cocking my head to the side he smiles and says he just wanted to take one more look at me before leaving. My first reaction was a big smile, soon followed by a warmed heart and a tingly feeling inside. After closing the door another feeling hits me, a sad feeling. Not because he had to leave but the way his eyes stared at me, it was almost as if he were doing it for the last time. The overall feeling is very difficult to explain and within seconds I talk myself out of that craziness. I will be seeing him in two days at work, what am I thinking?

Chapter Twenty-Six

Shelby

Today is difficult. I was supposed to be on a plane to meet Vincent in New Orleans but instead, I'm just sitting on my couch. This was a trip I was really looking forward to and knowing Michelle is there in my place almost kills me. This is the first time I've felt a jealous rage towards her and to be honest, it's unwarranted. She is his wife, she has every right to him, but it still hurts me. Vincent texted me before he left his house, letting me know he'd be in touch as much as possible but it may be a little difficult.

So here I am, alone again, sitting in my apartment. A few friends of mine invited me out tonight but to be honest, I just wouldn't be much fun to be around, so I declined. Tonight, it will just be me, a pint of ice cream and a few glasses of wine.

The next day I try to keep a little busy by helping my sister sort through her garage in preparation for a yard sale.

"Oh my god Kristi, how do you accumulate so much crap?" I ask, after filling three boxes of various things.

"I don't know, it just happened I guess," she replies. "Hey if you see anything you want, just take it."

I doubt I will take anything. Kristi and I have completely different tastes and I don't like to clutter my place with useless things. I end up staying for dinner and I'm glad I did. The last thing I need is another lonely night by myself, craving the man I love. Speaking of Vincent, unfortunately I haven't heard much from him but it doesn't surprise me. For a moment I wonder how long I can go on like this. When we are together, it's perfect, or as close to perfect as it can be. I'm happy, in love and feel so desired. It's the lonely nights that make me question everything about us. If we continue our love affair in this way I will always be second in his life. Would he ever consider leaving his wife? He's so unhappy, he's said so many times. Then again, I don't want to be the reason for their end. I know it would cause a lot of distress, especially with his kids. Even though they are grown and have their own families I still wouldn't want them to despise me for breaking up their mother and father. Why does this have to be so difficult?

Today is Sunday and reflecting on this weekend, I hardly recognize myself. I need to get myself out of this rut. Fact is, no one has ever loved or cared about me the way Vincent does. One look into his eyes and I feel like I'm home, a feeling I've never had with anyone else. In any case, I will see him tomorrow at work and I can't wait.

Vincent

Michelle and I have finally made it back home and to tell the truth, I'm exhausted. Not so much from the seminar, more from all of the running around we did in the evenings. Overall, we had a great time together and it almost reminded me of a time when we were happy. Even though our happy moments are very rare, there is always a small glimmer of hope that things will magically fix themselves. Either way, I'd be caught in the middle of a problematic situation I created. If I focus on my marriage, I would have to say goodbye to Shelby, which I know I can't do. If things stay the way they are, with Shelby and my relationship staying a secret, I continue betraying my wife. Then there's another thought. What if I end my marriage to be with the woman I love, the woman I desire? Honestly, I've dreamed of this more than I'd like to admit, but there is a part of me that holds back. She's much younger than me, things are great now but at one point I won't be able to keep up with her, it's a fact.

"Vince, can you just take the suitcases to the laundry room for me?" Michelle asks, bringing me back to reality.

"Of course, honey," I reply, picking up the suitcases.

The next day I walk into the office and there she is, wearing that unforgettable smile. God she's everything to me.

"Good morning Mr. Steele," Shelby greets me. "Would you like some coffee this morning?"

"Good morning Shelby," I reply. "Yes please. That sounds wonderful."

As she walks to the coffee maker to prepare my cup, John walks up with a big grin on his face.

"So Vince, how was the trip?" he asks, nudging me with his elbow. "Bryce said the Mrs. joined you this time."

"It was a good trip," I start, not wanting to have this conversation in front of Shelby and walking into my office with John in tow.

Once in my office John mentions something about a vacation he would like to take with his wife and asks if Michelle and I would join them. To tell the truth I am not in the least bit interested, but I know his wife will have been in contact with Michelle about it by the time I get home from work today. Telling him we will think about it, Shelby walks in with my cup of coffee.

"Thank you, Shelby," I say as she set it on my desk.

"My pleasure, sir," she smiles before walking out of the door.

"Now that is one woman I would love to have my way with," John whispers. "If I weren't married that is."

I feel myself tense up, hating the thoughts going through his head about the woman I'm in love with. He continues blabbering about who knows what for about another ten minutes before finally leaving my office and I lean back in my chair, rubbing my temples. I need to make sure Michelle doesn't want to go on this trip, there's no way I can spend a week with him. I will need a vacation just to recover.

The week is almost over and there's been zero opportunity for Shelby and I to spend any time together. Sure, we've snuck in the occasional kiss here and there, but with Michelle spending more time at home, it's so difficult to get away. Tomorrow is Friday and come hell or high water, I'm going to see her after work.

Picking up my phone, I decide to send Shelby a message to see if she has a few minutes to spare to come into my office. Not even two minutes later there is a knock at my door and I say come in. My eyes connect with hers and I get up from my chair, walking towards her.

"Lock the door behind you," I order and she grins and does so.

"Vincent, what do you have planned," she asks, giving me a curious look.

"Well, what I have planned will have to wait until tomorrow after work, but here's a little preview," I say, grabbing her by the waist and kissing her passionately.

My hands travel down, gripping her bottom as my tongue discovers her neck, making her hold back a moan. Running my hand up her leg and under her skirt, my fingers peel away her panties when suddenly there is a knock at the door. Shelby immediately jumps back, giving me a concerned look and I hand her a file. Walking over to the door I quietly unlock it and run back to my chair.

"It's open, come in," I say and once the door flings open I can't believe my eyes.

"Grandpa," Libby yells, as she runs into my office, right past Shelby.

Looking at the doorway, there is Michelle, holding Jackson with a big smile. My eyes quickly study Shelby's reaction, as Libby falls into my arms. I would say shock would put it mildly.

"Michelle, what a surprise," I smile and Shelby seems to be stuck in her spot, not knowing what to do.

"We were in the area and the kids wanted to see grandpa," she begins. "Oh Shelby, it's great to see you again."

"Mrs. Steele, the pleasure is all mine. You have some adorable grandkids."

"They really are," Michelle beams. "Libby is definitely a grandpa's girl though. She's been fascinated with Vince ever since she was a tiny baby."

Libby jumps off my lap and hands Shelby a piece of paper she's been holding in her hand, telling her she drew it earlier that day. Shelby bends down, studying the picture and telling her she did a wonderful job. I really feel as if I'm sweating bullets right now, less than five minutes ago I was seducing Shelby in the very spot Michelle is standing in right now.

"You're not working today?" I ask Michelle, and come to find out, she only had a half day.

"Well Shelby, it seems that Libby really has taken a liking to you," Michelle comments. "Do you babysit by chance?"

"No I don't, I'm sorry," Shelby informs her and Michelle exhales.

"Too bad, it would have been nice to find someone to give Vince and I a break sometimes."

Then there's an awkward silence for a moment until Shelby breaks it by excusing herself back to her desk. As the kids run around my office Michelle sits down and tells me about her day. Why did she have to come in today? I can probably count on both hands how many times she has ever set foot into this place. After about ten minutes she grabs the kids and kisses me goodbye, telling me we are going out to dinner tonight.

As soon as she is gone I walk over to Shelby's desk and I'm happy to see that everyone else is busy in their offices.

"I am so sorry Shelby," I whisper as I stand next to her.

"It's not your fault. I'm just glad Libby didn't recognize me," she replies and for a moment I am confused.

"What do you mean?" I ask.

"My brother in law works with your son. I met the family when I was at my sisters house for dinner."

"You're right. I completely forgot," I reply, now remembering everything and Shelby looks down.

"Are you okay?" I ask, taking notice that her body language has changed.

"Umm," she begins, pausing for a while. "Yes, of course."

Chapter Twenty-Seven

Shelby

When I get home from work I am still in shock about Vincent's wife surprising him in the office. We could have been caught, right then and there. Besides fear, I had another emotion consume me, deep regret. Regret that I ever started this affair. Seeing his grandkids run up to him and his wife smiling opened up my eyes. I can't do this anymore, I can't be the reason that a family could possibly get torn apart. I would never be able to live with myself. Even though I love him more than I could ever express, I will have to do the right thing and let him go. I know it will be hard and I know I will lose a part of my heart, but there is no way around it.

The next day I text Vincent, letting him know that I won't make it into work today. When he asks why, I just tell him I am not feeling well. I know he will come by here after work and I know I will break his heart, but I have to be strong. I was up all night, tossing and turning, trying to find another way, but there was none. All day I watch the clock and time seems to pass so slow. It's as if I'm dying a slow painful death and with each minute, the pain becomes worse. Lying in my bed I hear a knock and my body jerks immediately. Taking a deep breath, I get up and walk toward the front door. My eyes are a bit red from crying all night, knowing what lies ahead of me. Opening the door Vincent looks at me and his eyes full of concern.

"Shelby, what's going on? Are you okay?" he asks, coming in and closing the door behind him.

"No," I say and he places his hand on my arm and I wish he hadn't touched me, because I feel as if I am about to fall apart.

"What's wrong love? Tell me. Whatever it is," he says, pulling me over to the couch and setting me down.

"I," I begin, as he sits down next to me, holding my hand. "I...I can't do this anymore Vincent."

"Can't do what?" he asks, he has no idea.

"We have to stop seeing each other," I manage to get out, even though I am choked up.

"What?" he says, eyes widened.

"Yesterday, when your wife came into the office I realized that we are doing a terrible thing. I don't want anyone to get hurt and if we continue, it will be inevitable. At one point, it's going to come out and I don't want to be the reason for hurting someone in that way," I confess and he just stares at me, shock written all over his face, but still holding my hand. "It's not just that. Knowing that you will never come home to me and us not being able to have a real relationship is slowly killing me inside. I love you so much and the thought of never being able to have the life I want with you is something I can't live with."

"I love you Shelby. Please, I don't want to live without you," he says, breaking my heart with the pain I see in his eyes.

"And I love you Vincent. I love you more than words can say, but we can't go on like this. You know it as well as I do."

"I can't lose you," he replies and I have to stay strong.

"Are you planning on leaving your wife?" I ask, knowing fully well that he won't.

"Shelby, it's so complicated. I can't ju-"

"I don't want you to leave her. At least not for me. If you leave her, do it because you're ready and it's what you want. I'd never want you to choose. The two of you have been together for so long and I don't know if your relationship is repairable but I do know that with me in the picture, you will always feel as if you're in limbo. I want you to be happy. I don't want to see you stress, trying to divide your time between two women, it's not fair to anyone. Believe me, you will thank me for this one day."

"I don't know what to say," he pauses. "Do you regret us?

"Yesterday I did. Seeing Michelle put everything into perspective for a moment," I pause. "Now I know I don't regret us. The love you gave me is something I will cherish the rest of my life and you will live in my heart until the day I die. I don't have any regrets."

"My god," he says. "Why does this hurt so much?"

"I don't know. I suppose it proves how deeply we care for one another. I know it's going to take me a long time to get over you. I know I will never forget you."

"It's going to be so hard working beside you," Vincent sighs.

"It won't," I begin, pausing for a moment. "I will be giving you my written notice on Monday."

"What? You're leaving?" he says full of shock.

"I have to. You know as well as I that the two of us won't be able to stay away from each other. Trust me, it's for the best."

"I know," he replies with his head low. "So this is goodbye, the end of our chapter."

I feel a tear run down my cheek and close my eyes for a moment. Feeling Vincent's hand on my cheek, I open my eyes and see him staring back at me, his eyes glassy.

"I love you Shelby," he says, kissing my lips. "I always will."

Removing his hand, he gets up and a moment later he is gone and I immediately begin to cry, regretting what I've done. I know I did the right thing even though it seems to be tearing me apart right now. This is the end of our chapter.

Epilogue

Shelby

It's been a year since I've seen Vincent and I still miss him terribly. As time went by, I've tried to move on but a part of my heart still belongs to him, it always will. Sometimes I close my eyes and I recall the moment my life changed and a second later, he is standing in front of me, wearing that beautiful smile. I reach for him and an electric shock runs through me as I feel the palm of his hand on my cheek. Wishing we could stay this way forever. I fight with myself, knowing that as soon as I open my eyes he will be gone and I realize it was just another dream.

This happens more than I'd like to admit and it makes me wonder if I made a mistake leaving him. I still have his number in my phone, I couldn't get myself to delete it. In the past year there have been many times where I've written a text message and after staring at the screen for a long time, I ended up deleting it. We would just be in the same position we were in before, or worse, he may have not even replied.

Looking at the time I realize it's 6 pm and it's time to go home. I now work as a receptionist in an Urgent Care office about twenty minutes away from my apartment. I really do love my new job, it's very different from what I'm used to. After leaving Vincent's office I took a little time and went out of town to get away. I ended up staying with my brother for three weeks before returning to New

York. It's exactly what I needed, a clean break, away from everything that reminded me of him or us. Even though it was great being away, I still remember the day I walked into my apartment, reminiscing about all of the moments we shared here. Even a year later it still crosses my mind, but instead of being sad I look back and smile. I got to experience a love that some people will never find and I'm thankful that Vincent and I crossed paths.

Sitting in traffic I decide to stop by the coffee shop that's near the law office. As soon as I walk in, I remember the time Vincent and I were here and our talk about the photo wall. After ordering my coffee I wait, staring at the new photos on the wall. What a difference a year makes.

"Hello Shelby," a voice says behind me and my heart stops.

"Vincent? Oh my god, it's you," I reply feeling every emotion I thought I had locked away.

"I thought it was you. How are you?"

"I'm doing well, thank you. How are you?" I ask as the barista calls my name, informing me that my order is ready.

"Great," he replies as I reach for my cup. "Are you in a rush?"

"No, why?" I ask and he invites me to sit down with him in one of the leather sofa chairs.

I never thought I would see him again and now we are sitting next to one another. Within seconds I feel myself falling for him yet again, those eyes, that smile, just everything about him.

"How's Michelle?" I ask, feeling stupid for even asking.

"Michelle and I divorced," he replies and my eyes widen.

"What?"

"Yes. Everything was finalized four months ago," he pauses. "You leaving me was the best thing you could have ever done for me. Knowing you were gone, I focused on my marriage, and I mean really focused. Things were great for about a month and then it was the same as before, except we started fighting more. One day I sat down with her and after having an in-depth discussion, she said she's been unhappy for a very long time but didn't know how to tell me."

"Wow," I say. "So, she wanted the divorce?"

"She did, it was mutual. There was no fighting, it was very civil. We sold our house and I bought a condo in the city. It's a small two bedroom but perfect for me."

"Well, I am happy that you were able to find clarity and do what's best for you," I reply, smiling at him, but trying to hide my joy.

"Well, that's my story," he says pausing and looking directly into my eyes. "Are you seeing anyone?"

"I'm not," I reply and feel my heart race.

"Will you let me take you out on a date? A real date?" he says with a smile and I can no longer hide my excitement.

"I would love that," I reply and he takes my hand and holds it tight.

"On to our next chapter," he says, placing his hand on the back of my head and kissing my lips.

The End

Other Novels by CL Knopf

Unfold You

Bali

London

Links

www.facebook.com/clknopf

www.facebook.com/clknopfauthor

www.instagram.com/clknopf

www.twitter.com/clknopfauthor

www.facebook.com/groups/knopfsnightowls

https://clknopfauthor.wixsite.com/romance